BALA TAKES THE PLUNGE

Melvin Durai was born in Tamil Nadu and grew up in Zambia, where his parents worked as teachers. He went to America for college, earned a few degrees and landed a job at a daily newspaper in Pennsylvania, where he discovered his love for humour writing. He has written hundreds of humour columns, publishing them in newspapers and magazines in several countries, and gaining a loyal readership on the Internet. He and his wife, Malathi Raghavan, live in Winnipeg, Canada, with their three children, Lekha, Divya and Rahul. For more of his humour, visit his website: www.MelvinDurai. com.

BALA TAKES THE PLUNGE

MELVIN DURAI

First published in 2010 by Hachette India
An Hachette UK company

SRD

A small portion of this book has been adapted from previously
published columns.

ISBN 978-93-5009-075-6

Hachette India
612/614 (6th Floor), Time Tower,
MG Road, Sector 28, Gurgaon-122001, India

Typeset in Georgia 10/12.3

Printed and bound in India by
Manipal Technologies Limited, Manipal

MIX
Paper from
responsible sources
FSC
www.fsc.org   FSC™ C104740

For Malathi

B. BALASUBRAMANIAM, B.E., HAD ALWAYS WANTED TO BE A director, but not quite the director he had become. He had wanted to direct Tamil movies and work with superstars like Rajinikanth and Kamal Haasan. What a thrill that would be, having the power to tell Rajini what to do: 'Sit here, put your legs up, allow me to get you some coffee, sir.'

He had dreamt of putting his name in the opening credits – 'Directed by B. Balasubramaniam' – and ending the movie with the initials ABC emblazoned across the screen, which everyone in India would come to recognize as 'A Balasubramaniam Classic'. The President of India would award him the Padma Bhushan and the Queen of England would make him an O.B.E., which would look far more impressive than just a B.E. Every other Indian, after all, seemed to possess a Bachelor of Engineering degree. India had become the world's biggest factory for engineers. The government was wisely considering a law requiring all engineering students to wear helmets, so they wouldn't hurt themselves when they fell off the conveyor belts. They were India's chief export to the developed world, finding themselves in countries like Australia, New Zealand, Canada and America, where Permanent Resident status was granted to anyone who could prove, beyond reasonable doubt, that they had a brain.

It would have been exceptional, of course, if Bala had earned his B.E. at IIT, the Indian Institute of Technology, where, even during the height of monsoon season, brainstorms were more common than rainstorms.

Bala's father, a civil engineer, had studied at the College of Engineering, Guindy (now part of Anna University), but never hesitated to sing praises of IIT. 'It is tops in whole world,' Appa would say. 'Even better than Masterji Seth's Institute of Technology.'

'*Massachusetts* Institute of Technology, Appa,' Bala would gently correct him. But Appa, as usual, was beyond correction.

'Masterji Seth's. That is what I said. It is not so good as IIT.'

Bala didn't come close to getting into IIT and he blamed this on the Indian cricket board. If they hadn't scheduled a series against New Zealand in the same month as his entrance exam, he would have studied harder and scored better. As it was, he kept getting distracted, much to his mother's dismay. 'You are ready, kanna?' Amma asked one morning, serving idlis and tomato chutney to Bala and his younger sister, Chitra.

'Not yet,' he replied. 'Appa's hogging the sports page.'

It was a miracle he got into engineering at all. He was granted admission to Sri Harichandran Institute of Technology in Chennai, named after its benefactor, a well-known businessman. Though only a few years old, the college was already well-regarded around the state, being affiliated to a college that was affiliated to Anna University. Its reputation got a further boost in Bala's third year, when administrators wisely changed its name to Thiru Harichandran Institute of Technology, compelling students to use the much-improved acronym of THIT.

Bala's dream of becoming a film director was put on hold, not permanently he hoped. He had mentioned this desire several times to his parents and each time they had splashed water on it, like it was a pesky ant climbing up the drain in the bathroom sink.

'Don't be stupid idiot, Bala!' Appa said one evening, his nostrils flaring. 'What film you are capable of making? Maybe you can make film about me. You can call it *The Civil Engineer* and show everyone how I am designing bridges that will be able to survive any amount of flooding. That would be blockbusting film, no?'

Bala wondered why Appa had become a civil engineer. There was nothing civil about him. If he made a film about Appa, he would have to call it *The Uncivil Engineer*. And he would never work with Appa – that would be unbearable. If he messed up, he would be called a 'stupid idiot', and if the film won an Oscar or another big award, he'd be elevated only to a 'lucky idiot'. No, it would be wiser to find an actor to play Appa, someone with a dimpled chin, receding hairline and moustache thick enough to be the actual hiding place of Osama bin Laden.

His mother was more gentle and gracious, but even she disapproved of her son's ambition. 'Look at the films today, kanna,' Amma said. 'The actresses – they are showing everything. What I am wearing as a blouse, they are wearing as a dress. One film I saw last year at the theatre – what was its name, I don't remember – this girl was lifting her sari while walking through a puddle and everyone could see her thighs! Chee chee! Did she not know she was being filmed? How people are paying good money to watch films like this, I have no idea.'

Bala was momentarily confused: Had Amma sneaked into the theatre without paying? No, she was incapable of breaking the law. She was the model of honesty. If a shopkeeper gave her an extra Rs. 10 in change, she would return it immediately. Appa, on the other hand, would pocket the money, saying it was only fair and citing at least three reasons: (1) He had been shortchanged at the very same store thirty-eight years ago; (2) the store was gouging its customers with high prices; and (3) it was up to him to balance out Amma's honesty. 'Do unto others,' he would say, 'as they would have done unto you.'

Bala's parents did not agree on many things, so he took it seriously when they both raised objections to his ambition. He wondered if it was worth the effort to go against their wishes and become a film director. They would never understand his career, never be fully proud of him. But on the positive side, he could get beautiful actresses to walk through puddles and show their thighs. He imagined himself directing a movie called *Monsoon Rain* in which all the actresses walked through puddles, lifting their saris high in the air. It would surely make a killing in the box office – but then it might also make Amma want to kill herself.

She had wanted him to be more practical about his career choice. 'I am not asking you to do anything in particular,' she insisted. 'You have many choices. For example, you can be cardiologist, neurologist, ophthalmologist, oncologist or gynaecologist. All good choices. You can even be gastroenterologist, like my brother.'

Bala's uncle was the only doctor in the family and everyone was either proud or envious of him. He worked from morning to night, both at a busy government hospital and thriving private practice, earning so much money that his wife, according to Amma and others, could live in the sari shop if she wanted to. Uncle and Aunty Balakrishnan had a cook, maid and driver (part of a growing staff), three cars in the garage and elegant furniture in their three-storey house, yet still had the means to take annual vacations in Europe and America and bring home expensive gifts. Thanks to their generosity or what Appa considered their constant and overwhelming need to exhibit their wealth, Amma was the proud owner of a cupboard full of shiny white Corelle dishes. She treasured them so much, she couldn't bear to put any food on them. Even on special occasions like Pongal and Deepavali, she couldn't justify using the dinnerware, partly because, as Bala surmised, the guests were mere commoners, not the prime minister or president or someone really important like Rajinikanth. Her family and friends were unworthy of fine ceramic; they were treated to fine stainless steel. If Rajini ever came for dinner, Amma would not only bring out her prized dishes, she probably wouldn't wash them afterwards either. The display in her cupboard would include a few signs, such as 'Rajini ate from this plate,' 'Rajini drank from this cup' and 'I poured sambhar from this bowl while staring at Rajini.' Amma often bragged that she was Rajini's 'biggest fan', upon which Appa would pat her on the back and say, 'Don't worry, Meena. You can always go on diet.'

At times, Bala wondered if Amma wanted him to become a doctor so he could go on shopping sprees to western countries and bring home more dinnerware that would never be used. He envied Balakrishnan Uncle's wealth, but didn't want a career that might require him to look down people's throats or, even worse, look up the other way. He didn't want to view blood and internal organs. He didn't want to have to cut people up, not unless they called him in the middle of the night. He was relieved that his father gave him the option of becoming an engineer. 'You are intelligent boy, so you must become doctor or engineer,' Appa said, forgetting how often he had called Bala a stupid idiot. 'You can go to Amricka and get exhalent salary.' (An exhalent salary, Bala thought, would be far more beneficial to his health than an inhalant one.)

If only he had been less intelligent, he could have become a film director. But with intelligence came responsibility – the responsibility to make all that grey matter matter. Engineering undoubtedly required vast amounts of intelligence. There were so many principles to learn, so many problems to solve, that Bala spent many a night racking his brain, searching for some unused portion of his cerebral cortex that he could tap for insight. It didn't help that the textbooks were dense and dry, with few illustrations and complicated writing, which the authors evidently hoped would produce greater analytical thinking from prospective engineers. Indeed, Bala had spent countless hours analyzing the various methods that could be used to torture the authors. According to his calculations, taking mass and gravity into account, a textbook dropped from a height of only one metre would cause considerable pain, as long as it fell on the right spot, which for male authors would have the added benefit of preventing any textbook-writing offspring.

Bala could think of several lecturers deserving of the same fate – it would make up for all the times in his life he had been hit or pinched in front of his classmates. These were lecturers who possessed advanced degrees and could take the material in any textbook – Machine Dynamics, Applied Thermodynamics or Manufacturing Technology – and make it far more boring. None could do it as well as Mr. Ganesan, who specialized in thermodynamics and was certainly a brilliant man. His brilliance was clear to Bala during the very first class, when he made the mistake of staring at Mr. Ganesan's bald head. He was so dazed that when Mr. Ganesan asked him to name the second law of thermodynamics, he started reciting Shakespeare. 'All that glitters is not gold, often have you heard that told...' Later, after his classmates had stopped teasing him, he took it upon himself to warn them to look away or shield their eyes when facing Mr. Ganesan. But unlike him, his friends Gopal and Thiru were filled with more admiration than apprehension.

'When his head is shining so much on the outside,' Gopal said, 'how much brighter it must be on the inside.'

'I can bet you he polishes it,' Bala said.

'I wish he would tell us what polish he uses,' Thiru said. 'I'd like to try it on my shoes.'

'Forget about your shoes,' Bala said. 'It's not your shoes that need brightening.'

If any student felt too bright, Mr. Ganesan's lectures served as a dimming switch. Nobody could keep up with them, let alone understand them. He spoke at a rate of three hundred words per minute, often while facing the blackboard. If the entire class took a nap, he wouldn't notice anything until halfway through his lecture. And even then, he'd go on lecturing, pleased that his students looked more absorbed than usual.

Bala somehow managed to get through Mr. Ganesan's class, largely with help from a booklet called *Thermodynamics Made Easy*. It was one of a series of 'made easy' booklets Bala had found at Amma's Zone bookstore, with titles such as *Engineering Graphics*

Made Easy, *Calculus Made Easy*, and *Brain Surgery Made Easy*. After buying the Thermodynamics booklet and surviving Mr. Ganesan's tests, Bala bought a dozen more booklets in various engineering subjects, just in case the publisher, Chandra Publications, went out of business. It was an investment in his future and he didn't want to take any chances. Concerned that a single booklet could be easily misplaced, he had them all bound together and wrote a new title on the cover: B.E. *Made Easy*. He felt only a trace of guilt about reading the booklets and depending on them to get through engineering. After all, his friends were hooked on them, too. Thiru had even gone to the temple and paid for a special puja to be performed in honour of Chandra Publications. But he and other students were careful not to take the booklets to college. The lecturers frowned on them. Mr. Ganesan would be outraged to see one of his students poring over *Thermodynamics Made Easy*. He would snatch the booklet and say, 'Thermodynamics is not supposed to be easy.' Then he'd call the editor of Chandra Publications and offer to write a booklet called *Thermodynamics Made Difficult*.

Getting through engineering college was more a case of survival than brilliant achievement. But it made Bala a success in the eyes of his relatives and, more importantly, turned him into what Appa had hoped he would become: an export-quality Indian. Not every Indian had skills that were in demand abroad. Varun, the son of the ironing lady, for example, would not be able to work outside Tamil Nadu, let alone India, though he was an artist whose work was seen and admired by millions of people. He specialized in painting pictures of the Chief Minister on walls and buildings. He had been doing it for almost two decades – even when she was out of power – and had lost count of how many portraits he had done, how many paint shops he had single-handedly kept in business. He had become so adept at painting her that he once finished an entire portrait while completely drunk. He claimed that his hands had been conditioned, through years of repetition, to follow a precise pattern of brushstrokes, that if he tried to paint any other politician, his hands would not cooperate. He imbued his portraits with such elaborate detail – you could even see the slight protrusion of the Chief Minister's right incisor tooth – that Bala often wondered if future generations would come to remember him as Varun van Gogh.

But Varun, for all his success, could not entertain thoughts of working abroad, not unless he took the Chief Minister with him. Even then, they would have to move to a country where wall portraits were permitted. In India, nobody seemed to care what happened to walls; in the view of the common man, a politician's portrait was at least a slight improvement over spit stains.

With his B.E. in mechanical engineering, Bala was confident he could work abroad without having to take a politician with him. Indeed, after gaining just two years of experience at a small manufacturing firm, he landed a job with an American company called FlexIt Inc., which made exercise equipment. It took him three months to receive his H-1 visa, permitting him to work in America, and another month to get his entry visa, most of it spent standing in line at the U.S. Consulate. In the aftermath of 9/11, the newly formed Department of Homeland Security had directed the consulate to suspend its appointment system, returning to a system that enabled officials to observe visa applicants during an extended period of stress. The line was so long, it meandered out onto the street, past a shopping centre and roadside eatery. So many people were joining the line that Bala wondered if some of them thought there'd be free food at the other end. But no, they were too well dressed, the women in elegant dresses, saris and salwar-kameez, the men in suits, button-down shirts and ties. Bala had deliberately chosen not to wear a tie. If his visa application was rejected, it would be too easy to hang himself. Not that he couldn't be happy in India – Indians were among the happiest people in the world, according to an international survey that had been prominently featured in major newspapers such as *The Hindu*. Bala had shown the article to Appa, who took a cursory glance, shook his head and said, 'What is this happiness they are writing about? You cannot pay the vegetable seller with happiness. You cannot say, "Look, I'm happy. I'm smiling. Now give me some beans and go."' As Bala shrugged, Appa added, 'I'm telling you, da, happiness cannot buy money.'

Bala wasn't happy standing there in the hot sun, amid an army of people, circles of sweat forming under his arm pits. He was hungry and wondered if he should pass Rs. 2 to the man at the end of the line and ask him to buy a bonda at the eatery and pass it back down the line. But other people were hungry too and he didn't want his bonda to shrink as they passed it down. He also remembered that one man had briefly stepped out of line to go behind a tree, which made him ineligible to pass bondas.

Bala was growing worried that his visa application would be rejected, that his father would be disappointed. Surely America would not allow all these people to enter its shores; at this rate, white people would be a minority within a decade and Varun would be able to paint a large portrait on the wall of the White House.

By the time Bala got inside the consulate, he was so famished, he found himself looking around for any free food. But none was visible, not even a measly murukku. The hunger worked in his favour, though, for he forgot to give his well-rehearsed 'America is the greatest country in the world and I thank God every night for its existence' speech. As he would come to realize later, kissing America's derriere did not score points with the consular officers; instead, it made them suspicious, wondering if the applicant had something to hide, perhaps an affinity for Communism or a history of bed-wetting.

He had to stand in several more lines before facing the final consular officer, a forty-something man who possessed a full head of white hair and the ability to look menacing while asking innocuous questions.

'How long do you plan to stay in America, Mr... how do you say your name?'

'Balasubramaniam, sir.'

'How long do you plan to stay in America, Mr... uh... Blue Submarine?'

'Three years, sir.'

'Then what?'

'Then I'll be coming back, sir.'

'To get a wife?'

'No, to get a job here, sir.'

'So you're not going to settle in America?'

'Most definitely not, sir.'

'Why not? Don't you think you'll like America?'

'I will, sir. But I also like India. My family lives here.'

'My family lives in America. That's why I like being

over here.'

Bala tried to laugh, but all he could manage was a nervous chuckle.

'Do you know how to fly a plane?'

'No, sir.'

'Have you ever thought of taking flying lessons?'

'No, sir. Never in my life.'

'Do you know anyone who has ever thought of taking flying lessons?'

'No, sir. Even driving is a challenge in my family.'

'Where did you get your degree from?'

'SHIT, sir. I mean, THIT. Thiru Harichandran Institute of Technology.'

'What was your favourite subject?'

'Manufacturing Technology, sir.'

'So you like to make things?'

'Yes, sir, I do.'

'Have you ever made a bomb?'

'No, sir, never. I like to make useful things.'

'Some people would say that bombs are useful.'

'Not me, sir. I say that bombs are useless. Totally useless.'

'What about the bombs that America is dropping on Iraq?'

Bala hesitated. 'Useful, sir. Very useful.'

The officer asked a few more questions, then nodded, ever so slightly. 'Okay then. I'm approving your visa. Good luck in America, Mr... uh... Bald Superman.'

Bala was so thrilled when he left the consulate, he gave a thumbs-up to the people still waiting outside and told the bonda seller to keep the change. He suddenly realized what H-1 must stand for: Happy One. He was indeed happy to have a visa. He could work in America for at least three years and, if he couldn't stay longer, would still have enough money to return to Chennai and start his own engineering firm.

But things worked out better than he had expected. FlexIt was pleased with his work and sponsored him for permanent residency. A week before his fourth anniversary in America, he was the proud owner of a green card. He couldn't believe it – he could stay in America as long as he wanted. In five years, he would be eligible for citizenship, though the idea of giving up Indian citizenship did not sit well with him. He was hoping to become a dual citizen, pledging allegiance to two great countries, enjoying Hollywood and Kollywood, wearing dress pants with chappals, spreading peanut butter and jelly on his chapattis.

He had already been promoted twice and was earning an annual salary of $80,000. His parents were extremely proud: Appa was telling everyone that his son was earning three lakhs a month, while Amma was making space in her cupboard for more dishes.

Bala was quite pleased with his status at work. He didn't direct films for a living, but he was at least a director of some sort – Director of Design Engineering. It was a good title, better than Chief Design Engineer or Manager of Design Engineering. But he didn't want to get carried away with titles. He knew that companies handed out titles to keep employees happy. Titles did not cost the company anything, aside from the extra space needed in the office for the employee's head. Even so, he knew his parents and relatives were delighted to hear he was a director, never mind that FlexIt was a small company, with all the manufacturing being done in China. The title imparted a great amount of prestige. When he saw the words 'Director of Design Engineering' engraved on the silver plate on his door, it made him feel important and made others think he was important too.

He had chosen not to put his name on the door. It would draw attention from the title and might also intimidate people. Visitors to his office saw his name soon enough. It was on a special double-length name plate on his desk:

BILL BALASUBRAMANIAM

It had a nice ring to it, not unlike Robert Redford, Sushmita Sen and Mickey Mouse. His real name, appearing in full on his passport and other official documents, was Balasubramaniam Balasubramaniam, or, as his college friends used to joke, Balasubramaniam². Soon after Bala's birth, his parents had consulted a guru to help choose a good name for their son and the guru found it auspicious for the baby to carry the name of his father, perhaps because, as Bala would later conclude, the guru had misplaced his book of Tamil names.

The guru apparently couldn't foretell what life would be like for a man who went to America with two 15-letter names. It was not a problem in India though. Indians were used to long names. Among his engineering batch-mates, Balasubramaniam was only the third longest name, trailing Hariharaputhrapillai and Venkatasubramaniam. Bala was pleased that one of the girls had a name as long as his: Supriyadarshini. She was a beautiful girl, with long flowing hair, and all the boys enjoyed saying her name. Bala spent many a class period staring at her and fantasizing about whispering her name into her ear.

In America, however, such names caused trouble. Bala quickly learned that only a few Americans would be able to say his full name correctly. These were exceptional individuals – prodigies who possessed the rare gift of Tamil pronunciation. Ordinary folks seemed to struggle merely to say 'Bala'. Many said 'Bayla' and 'Barley'. One of the directors at FlexIt had even asked Bala if he'd mind being called 'Bal'. Shaking his head vigorously, Bala wondered what would be next: 'Ba'. Every time someone said his name, they'd think of sheep. He didn't want to risk that, so he decided to adopt the name 'Bill', in honour of his favourite American president, Bill Clinton, who, as a former Rhodes Scholar and frequent visitor to India, would surely know how to pronounce Balasubramaniam.

2

IT WAS A BONE-CHILLING JANUARY DAY IN HARRISBURG, Pennsylvania, so cold that while shovelling snow that morning, Bala's fingers turned numb, his moustache felt stiff and a single question kept popping into his head: Was there any way to speed up global warming? How he wished he could have imported some Chennai weather – not the torrential rains that sometimes turned the streets into rivers but the intense sunlight that had inspired Appa, in his spare time, to develop a solar-powered clothes dryer. Amma had shaken her head as she watched Appa attaching the wires and cable to the solar panel on their terrace, beside the pots of flowering plants she tended. 'Why you need so many wires?' she asked. 'One long wire is enough to dry clothes.'

Bala was still thinking about the weather a few hours later as he sat sipping coffee in a second-floor boardroom overlooking the Susquehanna River, his chair positioned strategically next to the heating vent. He wished he could turn around and face the warm air, but he had a feeling the other managers would disapprove.

He wasn't fond of meetings, especially when he had little to contribute, but this one, he had to admit, was almost as exciting as watching a Test match. The senior management team – eight people in all, including Stewart MacDonald, the grey-haired president and majority owner – were discussing promotional ideas for a new product: The Flexerciser. Bala had helped develop the machine and was looking forward to seeing it appear on the market. He knew it would be popular in America. People were always looking for easy ways to work out and The Flexerciser was not merely an exercise machine – it was an exercising machine. It was designed to do all the exercising for them. All they needed to do was climb on, press the 'Start' button and hold on tightly (Bala hoped people would not be deterred by the 'climbing on' part). Like a bull at a rodeo, The Flexerciser would jerk up and down and emit gusts of hot air. Within ten minutes, they'd be sweating like a Texan in a curry shop.

The Flexerciser was this year's offering from FlexIt Inc., this year's gift to the exercise-challenged, this year's contribution to next year's yard sale.

'Picture this,' said John Reilly, the marketing manager. 'A 30-second commercial with Meg Ryan sitting on The Flexerciser, recreating that famous scene from *When Harry Met Sally*. We'll have millions of women convinced they can be in ecstasy while using the machine. Pass the doughnuts please.'

'I love it, John,' said Mike Mathwala, the chief financial officer, pushing the box of powdered and glazed Krispy Kremes down the oval table. 'Maybe we can sell it at convents and monasteries, any place where people aren't getting any.'

Laughter broke out, but Stewart quickly corralled it. 'Getting any what?'

'Uh... well... exercise,' Mike said.

'Let's get serious for a moment, people,' Stewart said. 'You know Meg Ryan would cost too much. Besides, we're a reputable company. We don't want to deceive people quite that much.'

Bala reached over a bowl of fake fruit and helped himself to a powdered doughnut.

'How much do we want to deceive them?' asked

Linda Powers, the human resources director.

'The usual amount, Linda. Enough to buy our machines, but not enough to keep using them. We want them to buy a new machine every year. That's what keeps our factory humming: repeat customers.'

Bala brushed the powder off his pin-striped trousers and helped himself to a glazed doughnut. 'So what's your idea, Stewart?'

'I think we should follow the same plan as last year and the year before, which has helped us become a household name among people weighing 300 lbs or more. We need another late-night, 30-minute infomercial featuring a former or minor celebrity, someone whom people recognize, but who won't demand a lot of money. Any of the kids from *The Cosby Show* would do.'

'Or the stars of *Cheers*,' said Brian Thomas, the sales and distribution manager. 'Perhaps even the cast of the top-rated TV show of the '90s: the O.J. Simpson trial.'

'What about the actors from *Fresh Prince of Bihar*?' Mike asked. 'Some of them are struggling to find work. We could get three for the price of one. Joe Ginder would probably be willing to work for food.'

Fresh Prince of Bihar was a parody of a popular show, running for a few seasons on Comedy Central.

'Ginder would be great,' John said. 'Our target market would identify with him. We can use "before" and "after" pictures. Before buying The Flexerciser: Fat and bald. After buying The Flexerciser: Fat, bald and broke. Ha ha.'

'I like Ginder,' Stewart said. 'I didn't watch *Fresh Prince of Bihar* all that much, but my kids were into it. They loved it.'

'Best sitcom ever,' Mike said. 'And I'm not just saying

that because the actors were Indian-Americans.'

'You young guys,' Stewart said, shaking his head. 'So quick to call something the best ever, as though you've seen them all. Bet you've never watched *The Honeymooners*.'

'Of course, I have,' Mike said. 'Last year in Hawaii. But then they saw me and pulled down their blinds. Honeymooners are no fun.'

Stewart chuckled. 'You young guys, always into reality shows. *The Honeymooners* was a classic, a fine show that will be appreciated several centuries from now, as soon as they defrost my cryogenically preserved body. *Fresh Prince of Bihar* was quite funny, I'll give you that. Joe Ginder made me laugh a few times, as did his co-star, Chris Namuti. Call his agent, John. See if he's available and willing to skip a few meals. The "after" picture would really sell our machine, especially if we can get Ginder to have a six-pack stomach, instead of a keg. If not, we'll have to try some special effects, such as putting Ginder's head on Oscar De La Hoya's body. But I'm not sure we can afford De La Hoya's body.'

'I'd like to afford his body,' John said. 'Just for one night.'

Everyone groaned. John was always making comments about men he liked. But no one had ever seen him with another man, not even just sharing a booth in a restaurant. Bala was even beginning to wonder if John was really a heterosexual who had yet to come out of the closet.

'If we can get Ginder, our sales will hit the roof,' Stewart said. 'Especially since I read some good news in today's paper: 80% of Americans are now overweight. That's according to a national survey sponsored by the United States Food and Agriculture Trust (USFAT).'

Stewart opened a copy of the Harrisburg *Patriot-News* and pulled out the Living section. On the front was a picture of several torsos on a sidewalk, along with the headline 'Our Overly Big City (O. B. City)'.

It was common practice for the media to avoid showing people's heads when illustrating obesity, hoping to give them some anonymity. Bala wondered if anyone ever saw these anonybods on TV and thought, *Hey, that butt looks familiar. I swear I've seen it somewhere before. Wait a minute… I think it's my wife's butt. I'd recognize it anywhere. But whose butt is that next to hers? Is it mine? Nah, it's too big to be mine. She must be having an affair. Wait till I get my hands on that guy. How dare he hang around with my wife! How dare he wear the same kind of jeans I do!*

Stewart pointed at the picture. 'There's only one downside to people getting so big: our machines need to get big too. Our competitors are already responding. LifeTrack is introducing a treadmill with two lanes. Obese people will love it, but it's also ideal for slim couples who like to exercise together. Fitness Unlimited is creating an exercise bed. No need to get up – you can just roll around in it. Even companies outside the exercise industry are taking advantage of the trend. General Motors is making a car with only one seat in the front and the steering wheel in the middle. Industrial Machine Corp. is coming out with a forklift designed for home use. You'll probably want to take that on your honeymoon, Bill, if you ever get married. It might be the only way to carry her across the threshold.'

Bala smiled, helping himself to another doughnut. He couldn't believe how fat people were getting. But it was good for the company, good for his job security. He wasn't keen on deceiving people – that's why he worked hard on designing the machines well. They were so strong, so durable that the company had even started giving consumers a printed guarantee: *This machine is guaranteed to last as long as your New Year's resolutions.* Bala knew that deceit was part of the business. If FlexIt didn't do it, its competitors would. The exercise industry had to keep up with the diet industry, which was continually producing drinks and supplements that overweight people could consume to melt away their fat, just in case they weren't consuming enough already. Most people got duped by the ads, which featured an ordinary person who had been transformed almost overnight. 'Poor saps,' Stewart loved to say. 'They think they're going to lose a lot of pounds, but they're actually going to lose a lot of dollars.'

Fitness clubs or gyms were no better. Their only guarantee was the monthly fee. They persuaded people to sign a long contract, knowing that some would never show up and those who did would spend most of their time taking breaks between intense two-minute routines of checking out the opposite sex. Or the same sex, as the case may be.

Bala enjoyed working in the exercise industry, partly because it was so competitive. Every year, dozens of new machines appeared on the market, most designed to make exercise easy. The people in the infomercials always looked like they were exercising for pleasure. Alas, when consumers finally stepped on the machines, they faced a sobering reality: they had to move their bodies themselves. That's why Bala expected The Flexerciser to be popular. It didn't help people burn many calories, but it did make them sweat, it did make them feel like they were exercising, which was a good start for most people. Next year's machine, which the company was already working on, would allow people to do a little more. They had tentatively called it The Flexserver. It was a walking treadmill equipped with not just a TV screen, but also a food and drink dispenser. The Flexserver would use what Stewart called 'people-friendly measurements'. Instead of being discouraged about walking for 30 minutes and completing only one-tenth of a mile, an overweight man could now call his friends and announce, 'Guess what? I just finished 6,336 inches! And a 16-inch pepperoni pizza too.'

Bala's parents were amused when he told them about all the exercise machines Americans were buying. 'Why they can't just go for a walk?' Amma said. 'Your Appa and I walk six kilometres a day. He walks five kilometres in the morning, I walk one kilometre in the evening.'

He explained to her that exercise machines were convenient. You could use them at any time of the day in the privacy of your home. You could wear whatever you wanted, even jog on a treadmill while wearing a sari. You didn't have to worry about people watching you or the weather outside or air pollution. 'What about when it rains in Chennai, Amma? You can't exercise then, can you?'

'Very true,' she said. 'I don't know how to swim. Maybe we too should get an exercise machine. When you come here, you can help us to get one.' As she spoke, Bala could hear his father's voice in the background: 'Electricity! It will use too much electricity!'

Bala called them every Saturday, around 10 a.m. in Harrisburg, 8 p.m. in Chennai. He spoke mostly to Amma, but it was like having a conversation with both. Appa was always ready to chime in, even when he didn't quite know the topic. Once, when Bala was telling Amma that his pants were getting tighter, probably shrinking in the dryer, she asked, 'Your waist – is it not getting bigger in America?' and Bala could hear Appa grumbling: 'What is he wasting? Tell him not to be wasteful.'

Bala was hardly ever wasteful. He saw plenty of waste in America and felt dismayed. At restaurants, people left piles of food on their plates, half-eaten burgers, barely nibbled potatoes and untouched vegetables, all bound for trash bins. They threw away food and other items at home too, including furniture that could be easily restored, glass bottles that could be easily recycled, and fruitcake that could be easily re-gifted.

'If only America could export its trash to poor countries,' Bala said to John over lunch one day.

'We do,' John replied. 'Don't you know that you can get *The Jerry Springer Show* in China?'

'I mean good trash.'

'We tried that. But most countries don't want our trash – they want our cash.'

Bala wondered what Appa would think if he came to America. He would suffer a heart attack when he saw all the waste. Even the gas-guzzling Sports Utility Vehicles (suvs) would put him in intensive care.

Bala could still picture the look of disbelief on Appa's face when they watched a documentary about transportation in America. 'How they can drive these big cars?' Appa asked.

'It's easy, Appa,' Bala replied. 'Just press the accelerator and steer. Most of them are automatics.'

Bala was tempted to buy an suv himself, but he kept hearing Appa's voice in his head, admonishing him not to 'waste' all that money. He had heard that stern voice all through his childhood. Appa never missed an opportunity to caution his children against wastefulness. At work, he was a civil engineer with limited power; at home, he was President and CEO of Waste Minimization Inc. 'Off the TV!' he would tell Bala. 'It is triple waste. You are wasting electricity, wasting time and wasting brain.' If Bala spilled juice or tea by accident, as he seemed to do at the most inopportune times, Appa would scream: 'You clumsy wastefool!'

Appa kept such close track of water and electricity usage that Bala was thankful that God had made oxygen invisible. Otherwise Appa would have restricted Amma and Chitra to two cubic centimetres per minute and Bala to one cubic centimetre, saying it was wasteful for Bala to inhale more, given his limited brain activity.

While children in America were apt to waste food – not just vegetables, but even the crust of a pizza or the crumbs of a cake – Bala and Chitra never did. Appa had taught them the importance of finishing everything on their plates, imparting his wisdom through seven simple words: 'If you don't eat, I will beat.'

Appa's voice, echoing in Bala's head, kept him from splurging on a fancy car or high-definition TV. Instead, he bought a Toyota Corolla and a 27-inch flat-screen Sanyo. He didn't get PIP (picture in picture). That would be like watching two TVs at the same time, wasting his brain at twice the normal rate. He bought a satellite dish, but only because he couldn't survive without cricket. Even his house was fairly modest: it had one living room, 1½ bathrooms and three bedrooms (his neighbour Mr. Cherian had five bedrooms, including a walk-in closet that Bala would have been comfortable in). Nevertheless Bala liked the house – it was small but cozy. And it was better than renting an apartment, which he had done for a few years. He didn't like having a landlord. That was like living under Appa. His landlord, Mr. Bratic, seemed to hold a lot of power over him. His title itself intimidated Bala. He was a landLORD while Bala was a tenANT. A lord was always more powerful than an ant. He could have stepped on Bala and not known it. These titles, Bala thought, went back to the early days in England when a certain lord of the manor allowed his land to be occupied by ten ants. Bala wished he could change the titles. He wanted to be a tenlord and have Mr. Bratic as his landant.

Getting away from Mr. Bratic was a big benefit of buying a house, but so was getting more space to entertain friends. He liked having them over, particularly his childhood pal Thiru, who had also moved to America and lived an hour's drive away in Baltimore. They had started to watch American sports together, figuring out some of the rules themselves. Baseball was similar to cricket, except that the players were expected to spit more often. Ice hockey was an extremely fast sport; Bala and Thiru needed slow-motion replays to appreciate all the jabs and uppercuts. Football was the greatest sport of all – it allowed even overweight people to be athletes.

Bala invited his friends over at least once a week – and just as often visited their homes or joined them at clubs and restaurants. But he spent most nights alone at home, eating, reading and watching TV by himself. There was something lacking in his life, some void that needed to be filled. And the more he thought about it, the more he realized that at 29 he was ready to share his home and his heart, he was mature enough, responsible enough to get what was missing in his life: a dog.

He had seen hundreds of dogs in Chennai, but most were stray dogs, roaming the streets in search of food and shelter. He didn't really appreciate dogs in his childhood; the closest he came to making a connection with one was when a stray dog barked at him and, in the wisdom of youth, he barked back. That dog left a lasting impression on him, but unfortunately it was with its front teeth. His ankle hurt so much, he forgot to bite back.

But the memory of that incident had long faded when he came to America. He was surprised to see what an important role American dogs played in their owners' lives. They went on walks with their owners, jogged with them, played Frisbee with them, fetched tennis balls and newspapers for them, sat upright in cars so their owners could use car-pool lanes. At one wedding, the dog was the ring bearer; at another, it was the best man. Dogs had been trained to perform critical tasks: lead the blind, dial 911 in an emergency, fetch beer from the refrigerator. Bala was even surprised to see one dog, a beagle that lived down the street, exchanging a kiss with its owner. That's the ultimate sign of affection, he thought, for not everyone would be willing to put their lips on a scruffy old man.

Americans loved dogs to an extent he had not thought possible. They spent hundreds of dollars at the vet and even bought pet health insurance. They followed their dogs around with little bags and cleaned up after them, somehow convincing themselves that *they* were the masters. They treated their four-legged friends to doggie biscuits, doggie desserts and even doggie champagne. Some dressed their dogs in stylish clothes and were big proponents of 'doggie-style' – not just in the bedroom.

Bala wanted to have a similar relationship with a dog, wanted to participate in the human-animal bonding experience, so he took a trip to the local animal shelter and adopted the first dog that didn't bark at him. It was a black Labrador retriever, a 10-month-old male with a tail that wouldn't stop wagging, a mouth that wouldn't stop drooling. Hearing that President George W. Bush had a cat named India, Bala decided to name his dog America. It was a good way to honour his new country and confuse people all at the same time. When his neighbour Mr. Cherian complained about the dog's incessant barking, Bala said, 'What do you expect? This is America, not India.' When his neighbour on the other side, Mrs. Bunch, complained that a ripe tomato was missing from her garden and wondered where it had gone, Bala shook his head and said, 'Only in America. Only in America.'

He tried to do everything with America he had seen other dog owners do, except smooch. To his surprise, America was very intelligent and easy to train. He was a natural retriever, with an uncanny ability to fetch not only sticks and tennis balls but also dead rodents. Sometimes America would even chew a dead mouse or squirrel he had found, especially if the animal was still fresh – dead for less than five years. Dogs, it seemed, were not as particular as humans when it came to food expiry dates.

Bala also discovered that America could be trained to respond to any type of signal at feeding time. At first, he trained the dog to run for its food whenever he rang a bell. Then he got it to respond to a snap of the fingers. Finally he got it to spring into action whenever he said, 'Big red tomato.' America had an insatiable appetite and, unlike his namesake, never wasted a morsel of food. After eating his usual dinner of Nibbles 'n Grits, he always licked his bowl clean, almost as clean as Appa would have. Then the dog would sit upright in front of Bala and watch him finish his meal, often dripping so much drool on the floor that Bala was forced to get a mop from the closet and bop him on the head. It was always a gentle bop, not intended to hurt the dog but to shoo him away. Bala loved the dog and didn't want him to drown in his own drool. He loved the dog so much, he even got himself a new bumper sticker: 'God Bless America.'

America returned Bala's love tenfold – elevenfold if you included the times he got amorous with Bala's leg. But Bala realized that the dog couldn't give him everything. America was great for companionship and love, but intelligent as he was, his vocabulary was severely limited. Their conversations were always one-sided, though Bala appreciated having a companion who seemed to be such a good listener and never showed a hint of disagreement. He also appreciated that the dog didn't nag him about returning home late, didn't complain that the house was messy or that trash needed to be taken out, and, other than an occasional drink, didn't spend an eternity in the bathroom. Still, he wanted something more in a companion. He wanted to be able to cuddle on the couch, without being treated to regular blasts of canine breath. He wanted to enjoy a romantic candlelight dinner, without having to set the plates on the floor and shield the candle from the stream of drool. He wanted to play a board game at night, without his partner constantly smelling the game pieces to see if they were edible.

He had enjoyed his single life and was afraid to give it up – would he still be able to watch sports on weekends or eat cornflakes for dinner? – but he also knew it was time to think about the next phase. He was feeling increasing pressure from home to settle down and start a family. None of his relatives, thankfully, had asked him the annoying question, 'When are you getting married?' But they had used the same five words, in different combinations.

Balakrishnan Aunty: 'When you are getting married?'

Cousin Rahul: 'When getting married are you?'

Ravi Uncle: 'You are getting married when?'

These days, he couldn't speak to any of his relatives without the subject of marriage coming up. He was beginning to wonder if it was worth calling them at all. Surely it would be cheaper to just email them the same reply: 'I'm an engineer, not a psychic.' And just in case they didn't get the message, perhaps he would also send them Rajini's words from the movie *Baasha*: '*Naan oru dhadavai sonna nooru dhadavai sonna madhiri.* (If I say it once, it is like I say it a hundred times.)'

His parents were behind these queries, he was sure. Every time they got together with friends and relatives, his marriage was doubtless a hot topic. He could picture Appa's eyes lighting up as he raved about Bala's qualifications, embellishing them to the point where Bala wasn't just an engineer with a green card who was 'minting money' – he was also the director of a multi-million-dollar corporation that played a major role in determining the health of Americans and, as such, could also be considered a doctor. Such a description was enough to excite parents of the most eligible brides in Tamil Nadu, some of whom possessed qualifications that had also been suitably doctored. Amma, for her part, wanted nothing more than to serve as the chief screener in this contest, making sure that only the most deserving, fair-skinned candidates would gain an audience with her perfect son, have a shot at becoming her daughter-in-law and perhaps, if they played their cards right, inherit her Corelle dishes.

'You don't worry, we will arrange everything,' Amma said, trying to reassure Bala. 'Just buy your ticket and come and see the girls. We will find some nice, sweet ones that are not spoiled.' Her words caused him to cringe, because the last time he had heard his mother use the phrase 'nice, sweet ones that are not spoiled', she had just returned from the market with a bag of mangoes.

'Leave it to us – you have more important things to worry about,' Appa said, as though Bala was trying to get his cable hooked up, rather than himself. 'We know what you want. We will find good girl for you.' But the idea of his parents finding a girl for him did not sit well with Bala, for he had decided that what he really needed, what he really desired, was a *woman*. Girls were immature, lacking in confidence and direction, unable to express their individuality. Women, on the other hand, had decided what they wanted in life and weren't afraid to state their opinion, even if it meant disagreeing with a high-earning engineer/doctor. He knew such women existed. He had seen them on *Oprah*.

It was clear to Bala what he had to do: find a suitable bride for himself before his parents did. He didn't want to be pressured to settle for one of their choices, just as he had settled for a career in engineering. They were eager to take the weight off his back; he was afraid they'd drop it on his feet. It was inevitable that they'd disagree with or misunderstand his expectations. It had already happened: 'I'd like a wife who is fairly slim,' he had once told Amma in a casual conversation. 'No problem,' she said. 'We will find you a bride who is fair and slim.'

Time was not on his side. He was now less than a year away from the big 3-0 and, with the time difference, even closer in India. Unlike women, he didn't have a biological clock. But he could still hear something ticking. He wondered if the next time he flew he could get airport security to check all his parental baggage.

3

THE NEWS WAS NOT GOOD AT WORK. JOHN HAD SENT A MEMO to all the senior managers: 'Joe Ginder has turned down the opportunity to appear in our infomercial, though it would have been his biggest acting role in years. According to his agent, he is not interested in losing weight, calling it an out-of-date practice. He is happy to be a round man, especially since his wife is a good cook and he doesn't want to disappoint her. He is also getting plenty of endorsement opportunities from the food industry and prefers ads in which he is eating rather than exercising. It's a good thing we made a list of alternative endorsers. I checked with Stewart and we've decided to pursue Pablo Fromrio.'

Pablo, an immigrant from Brazil, had gained fame in 2000 when presidential candidate Al Gore mentioned him in a debate, accusing one of his opponents, John Sperry, of employing an 'undocumented pool guy'. Pablo, who had entered the country illegally through the Mexican border, became a household name almost overnight, known to everyone as 'Pablo the Pool Guy'. He appeared on every TV talk show, published an autobiography and, for a few months, even hosted his own show on CNN called 'Politics and Pool Tips'.

'The only problem,' John's memo continued, 'is that he's tall and slender, so we may have to Photoshop the "before" picture instead of the "after". Perhaps Pablo can tell people he was depressed after his show was cancelled, spent his days at Taco Bell and gained a spare tyre and four hubcaps. He was unable to lose a single pound until The Flexerciser came along. I am checking with Joe Ginder's agent to see if we can use his body.

And no, I do not want it for personal use.'

Bala was concerned. It was important to get a good endorser, someone who could appear on TV and hard-sell The Flexerciser to millions of people, someone who could do as well as last year's endorser, Annika Le Vinsky, a former political aide of French descent who came to national prominence in 1997 when President Clinton asked her to serve under him. Le Vinsky was a perfect pitchwoman for FlexIt, having lost 30 pounds since her days of providing personal service to the president. Dressed in tights to accentuate her svelte figure, she did a masterful job of selling the previous machine, The Flex-appeal, which, as luck would have it, was well-suited to her talents: It allowed people to burn calories while on their hands and knees. It was like a combination treadmill and elliptical trainer, requiring users to assume a position that Le Vinsky, trying to change her reputation, had somehow convinced millions of religious people was prayerful. 'If you have a busy schedule like mine, it's hard to find the time to pray and exercise,' she said. 'Now you can do both at the same time. Yes, for just 20 minutes a day, you can take care of both your body and soul.'

That marketing strategy, John's brainchild, was nothing short of brilliant, for it tapped into not only the religious fervour gripping a large swath of America but also a growing trend: multi-tasking. With their hectic lives, people just couldn't find time to do everything they wanted. Many were struggling to keep up with the demands of modern life. Some were even neglecting to do normal tasks, such as buying birthday gifts for their dogs. The solution, of course, was multi-tasking – tackling more than one task at the same time. Everyone seemed to be doing this to a certain extent, even Bala's dentist, who had developed the annoying habit of making small talk with his assistants, catching up on their lives, while drilling Bala's teeth. It made Bala feel like multi-tasking too: making small talk with the dentist, catching up on his life, while sneaking out without paying. Many people were even multi-tasking while driving their cars: eating sandwiches, sipping soft drinks, checking their email, speaking on their cell phones, applying makeup, flossing their teeth, reading newspapers and doing yoga. Any day now, Bala expected to see the inevitable newspaper headline: 'Multi-tasker sustains multi-fracture in multi-car accident. Police Chief calls him multi-stupid.'

Some forms of multi-tasking were obviously dangerous, but praying and exercising was surely not one of them, as Le Vinsky had amply demonstrated in the infomercial. Thanks to her virtuoso endorsement – it was unquestionably her best performance since her White House days – the company sold so many units of The Flex-appeal that it had to increase production by 50 percent at its factory in China and ask workers to temporarily skip breaks, meals and home visits. Workers who complied were promised enticing rewards: Not only could they keep their jobs, they could also keep, on interest-free credit, their very own Flex-appeal. It was contingent, of course, on the Chinese government allowing them to pray.

Bala and Mike – whose real name was Mukesh – had tried to persuade Stewart to open a factory in India. Bala knew the company would benefit greatly, but he also had a personal motive: he hoped the factory would employ his cousin Rajan in something other than beedi-smoking. But Stewart didn't want to take the risk, didn't want to confuse consumers. Americans, he said, had grown accustomed to getting their products from China and their customer service from India. An elementary school student, when asked to describe the American flag, would invariably write, 'The flag is called the Stars and Stripes. It consists of thirteen stripes, 50 stars, and a tiny "Made in China" label.'

China could make things cheaper than any other country, Stewart said. Chinese suppliers were always striving to give their American clients a good deal, always trying to be fair. Stewart recalled an occasion when flags had appeared at Wal-Mart bearing 53 stars. It seemed like a terrible mistake, but when management demanded an explanation, the Chinese supplier put them at ease. 'Why you complain?' he said. 'We give you good deal – 53 stars for the price of 50.'

If Le Vinsky had been available again, she would have given another boost to China. But having regained her fame and repaired her reputation, she had moved on to a more lucrative endeavour: giving massages at religious conventions. It was a continuation of the increasingly popular 'body and soul' theme. Bala hoped Pablo Fromrio would agree to endorse The Flexerciser and show as much enthusiasm as Le Vinsky. It was important for the company to continue to show sales growth. Otherwise heads would roll and Bala, playing a key role in developing each machine, might be the first to depart with just his torso. That was a disconcerting thought, especially since women were generally reluctant to marry a man who had lost his head.

He had been thinking about marriage a lot recently, so much that he felt compelled to get on the Internet and do a search for Chandra Publications. They had helped him get through engineering college; perhaps they could help him again. But Chandra's online catalogues failed to give him what he wanted. There was no booklet called *Marriage Made Easy*.

He went to Ebby's Independent Bookstore in downtown Harrisburg and found an entire section of how-to books, many of them narrowly targeted, including a blue paperback with a title that immediately caught his eye: *How to Find the Perfect Mate in 30 Days or Less With No Help From Your Parents in India*. The book was touted as a 'Bestseller in Australia, Canada, Singapore and parts of New Jersey'. Bala decided to buy the book, as well as several prize-winning books, including *Midnight's Children* by Salman Rushdie, *The Interpreter of Maladies* by Jhumpa Lahiri, and *The God of Small Flings* by Bill Clinton. He planned to read a couple of the books and display the rest prominently in his living room, as he had seen many people do. Displaying books was better than displaying degrees. No one would accuse you of being pretentious, no one would find out which second-rate college you attended. Books made you look smart and literate and cultured. Not everyone had the good taste to buy Rushdie, not everyone could appear to have read him. Bala, determined to be part of the exclusive Rushdie Readers Club, took the novel to the couch and spent a couple of minutes dog-earing it. Then he took it to the kitchen and spilled a few drops of curry on random pages. Finally he snapped the cover back, so it didn't look so tight, and placed the book on his coffee table. It would have been cheaper to buy a used Rushdie at a book sale, but it was hard to find a Rushdie – everybody knew the value of having him in their homes. Some had entire collections of hardcover Rushdies on display in their living rooms. Every year or so, they would open one of their Rushdies to see if they had gained, with age and maturity, the intellectual capacity to understand him, then drop their heads in shame and go back to reading their Grishams.

Bala hoped he could impress a few women with his fine taste in literature. Among his friends, Mike was the most impressed, at least initially. Visiting one evening with Thiru, he picked the Rushdie off the coffee table and thumbed through it to check for authenticity – perhaps it was a Grisham disguised as a Rushdie, what closet fans of pulp fiction referred to fondly as a Grishdie. Finding no ordinary prose, Mike shook his head in disbelief. 'You read Rushdie? Wow!'

Bala shrugged, trying to keep a straight face. 'Doesn't everybody?'

'I didn't realize you were so... so... you know, cultured.'

Thiru burst out laughing. 'Don't let the book fool you. Bala doesn't read Rushdie. Before you can read Rushdie, you need to be able to read Archie. Bala will have a hard time reading *Rushdie Made Easy*. He will need to buy *"Rushdie Made Easy" Made Easy*.'

'Don't listen to him,' Bala said, handing Mike a can of ValueTime ginger ale. '*Midnight's Children* is a great book. It's a horror story about children who go out at midnight and terrorize people. It made me tremble so much, I spilt some curry on it. Rushdie won the Booker Prize for it, you know.'

'That's how he attracts all those hot babes,' Mike said. 'He may not be a looker, but he's got a Booker.'

Bala wished he could write a book that would impress women. Instead, he would have to impress them in other ways. The problem with American women was that they were not easily impressed with a man's profession, unless he was a professional athlete, actor or musician. And the problem with Indian women was that most of them were in India. Going to India to get married meant involving his parents and he wanted to avoid that, if at all possible. But there were so few Indians in the Harrisburg area, even if you included the kind that Columbus discovered. Bala knew what the problem was: Indians, when they came to America, spent too much time on recreation and not enough on procreation. The few times Bala had spotted an attractive Indian woman in her twenties, she was either taken or being taken – some guy, usually her father, was taking her somewhere.

As for Indian women living in other parts of America, it wasn't easy to make a connection with them. Bala would have to either place a matrimonial ad or reply to one. Or he could attend one of those networking conferences for Indian professionals, where he'd have a chance to see attractive, qualified, confident women talking to attractive, qualified, confident men.

Meeting American women would be far easier, of course. They were all around him and many of them, he was starting to notice, were quite alluring. The blonde clerk at Gigantic Foods near his home was a few degrees beyond gorgeous. He always went to her checkout, unable to resist doing some checking out. Her name was Brooke – she wore a name tag, and he had somehow managed to pull his eyes off her face long enough to read her first name. If there was a nuclear disaster or some other calamity, he'd owe his life to her, for she was the reason his spare bedroom was packed with food. Their relationship had reached a milestone the previous week: She didn't ask him the usual question. She remembered that he preferred plastic. It was a magical moment, one he would have recorded in his journal, if he kept one. As she dropped his canned peas into a plastic bag, she made eye contact with him and he realized he was no longer just another customer – he was a man whose preferences were stored somewhere in that pretty head. He wondered if any other customer had made such a connection with her.

But then there was the matter of age and accomplishment. She looked like she was eighteen or nineteen. She was probably a college student at best, with only a high school diploma to her name. What would Amma say? How would he convince his parents she was the right woman for him? He'd have to choose his words carefully: 'You'll really like her, Amma. You can tell all your friends that your son has found himself a bride who is extremely fair-skinned. So fair-skinned that she actually – you won't believe this – lies in the sun to get darker!'

He knew, of course, that Amma wanted his bride to be not just fair, but also a Tamil of the same caste, among a long list of criteria that would make the admissions director at Harvard Medical School feel like a total slouch. Accepting a daughter-in-law of another race would be like – god forbid – mixing Pfaltzgraff with her Corelle. Bala had noticed that even in America, many parents who considered themselves open-minded and unprejudiced, who patted themselves on the back for having friends and neighbours of other races, seemed to yank the welcome mat whenever their sons or daughters talked about marrying one of 'those people'. While sitting at Great Wall Restaurant one evening near a father and son of Chinese descent, Bala overheard a conversation that made him realize how significant racial differences are.

'Why can't I date Tanya?' the teenaged boy asked.

'She has a nice face, nice body and nice music collection. What more could I want?'

The father shook his head in dismay. 'You're Chinese,' he said. 'You're not supposed to date someone named Tanya. You're supposed to date someone named Tan Ya.'

Bala hoped that if he hit it off with Brooke or some other American woman, he'd be able to convince his parents to accept her or at least pretend they did. They would be aghast at first, but perhaps as they got to know her, they'd realize it was for the better, especially since their son planned to stay in America, where mixed-race couples were so common, nobody stared at them for longer than a minute or so.

4

THE HOW-TO BOOK ADVISED BALA TO PUT HIS BEST FOOT forward, to make himself as attractive as possible. As the authors wrote, 'Even the most attractive people can look downright plain if they don't take care of themselves, if they don't dress well, stay in shape and make regular visits to their plastic surgeon.' The first step, they said, was to look at yourself in the mirror and evaluate your strengths and weaknesses, being as objective as possible. Bala didn't have a full-length mirror at home, so he went to Wal-Mart and bought one, then set it up in his spare bedroom against a stack of Corn Flakes boxes. He stared at the mirror for a few minutes, scratched his head, stared some more, scratched some more. Where were these weaknesses they were talking about? He couldn't seem to find any. He tried squinting. Still no weaknesses. He wiped his plastic-rim glasses, but that didn't help either. According to the book, everyone had weaknesses, but where were his? His strengths were easy to spot – they stood out like a group of Indians at a country music concert. He was a handsome man with a strong chin and pronounced cheekbones. He possessed long eyelashes and, despite his dentist's best efforts, every one of his teeth. He smiled at his reflection, showing as much enamel as possible. Which woman would be able to resist that?

Perhaps his weakness was an inability to spot any weaknesses. But what if he really didn't have any? What if he, Bill Balasubramaniam, had been chosen by God to be the world's first perfect man? Perhaps Amma was right: her son *was* faultless. He moved closer to the mirror, took his shirt off, puffed out his chest. Oh no! He *did* have a weakness. His nipples were showing! He had not grown enough chest hair. Why did men have nipples anyway? So they could practise caressing them? So they could get to know their feminine side? Perhaps it was to remind them that women could do something they couldn't. Whatever the reason, he didn't want his nipples to be so conspicuous. He grabbed a hairbrush and tried to push the strands of chest hair over his nipples, but they kept springing back. He wondered if he should try some hairspray. That would probably do the trick, as long as he didn't allow any women to run their fingers over his chest – they might wonder if one of his ancestors was a porcupine.

Having spotted one weakness, he was willing to consider the possibility, however remote, that he might have others. He turned sideways, somewhat cautiously, and looked in the mirror again. Oh no! His stomach was protruding, much further than seemed natural. He wasn't expecting this – to look like he was expecting. This was surely a weakness, though he could still squeeze into his Size 32 Levi jeans – the ones he bought in college – as long as he didn't pull them all the way up. It was so easy to gain weight in America. Everywhere he looked, there was food. At his workplace, cookies, doughnuts and cake were always appearing. And then, just as suddenly, they were disappearing. At restaurants, food was served in huge portions, often at all-you-can-eat buffets. One evening, Bala and Thiru ordered chicken and mashed potatoes at Horse's Family Restaurant; the chicken came in a bucket, the mashed potatoes in a trough. They ate continuously for more than an hour, until their stomachs were about to burst, then packed the remaining two-thirds for a snack for America.

Bala had read in *Health&Fitness* magazine that it was wise to eat five or six meals a day. Smaller, more-frequent meals make your body more efficient, allowing it to burn extra calories, a leading nutritionist had said. But what the nutritionist didn't realize was that once Bala's body started eating, it was hard to get it to stop. It helped, of course, that Bala didn't eat certain types of food that were popular in America. He didn't eat crabs and lobsters, which looked like the world's biggest insects. Grocery stores kept these 'insects' in aquariums, so people could get to know them before they ate them. That seemed strange to him, as did most of the items available in the Meat Department. He made it a point to avoid beef, pork, lamb and any other meat that came from four-legged creatures. He once tried mutton, but only after his friends convinced him it came from a mutant three-legged sheep. He had grown up a vegetarian, but had developed a taste for chicken in America, unbeknownst to his parents. Amma was such a strict vegetarian, she wouldn't even want to try horseradish, just in case. He wondered how he would tell her about his new eating habits. Perhaps he would wait until he was ready to marry an American, then give Amma the related news all at once: 'I'm sorry to tell you this, Amma, but I've taken a liking to American chicken – and also an American chick.'

Bala's co-worker Brian couldn't understand why so many Indians insisted on being vegetarians. 'Some of them are starving,' he said. 'Why can't they just eat their freakin' cows?'

Bala could picture millions of Indians kissing Brian's feet and saying, 'Thank you so much, great guru. We never thought of that. Because of lack of food, our minds were not working properly. Now, instead of searching for rice and dal, we can eat steak, hamburgers and pot roast. We'll never be hungry again. And we'll erect thousands of statues in your honour.'

Bala informed Brian that the vast majority of Indians, for religious and other reasons, did not consider cows as potential meals. 'It would be similar to asking Americans to eat dogs,' Bala said.

'In that case,' Brian said, 'we'll send Indians our dogs if they send us their cows.'

Bala laughed, though the idea seemed ludicrous, especially since no Indians, as far as he knew, had developed a taste for dogs. Most didn't even care for hot dogs. Besides, if any country should be exporting dogs, it was India. There were so many dogs in India, you could travel the entire length of the country without finding a dry tree.

Trees were important, not just for India but also America, as Bala realized whenever he took him for a walk. The dog was like an overzealous gardener – he couldn't pass a tree without watering it. A little here, a little there, his generosity went far and wide. He was even more generous with fire hydrants, perhaps believing they were undernourished trees. Nevertheless, Bala enjoyed these long walks, partly because strangers, seeing him with America, were far more likely to smile at him or greet him. Some even complimented him: 'Nice dog!' When he and America passed another dog and owner along the street, the other dog would often bark at America. It was obvious to Bala what the dog was saying: 'Nice human!' All the compliments were great, but the best part about going for walks was the exercise. It was the only regular exercise he got. At other times, he seemed to be always sitting: sitting in his office, sitting in his car, sitting in the bathroom. At least in India, many people squatted in the bathroom. Squatting was better than sitting. Sitting, of course, put less strain on your joints and made it easier for you to multi-task – Bala liked to read the business page of the newspaper while doing his business. But squatting put your body in the perfect angle to get things moving, and it also improved your flexibility and helped you burn a few more calories. Squatting on a western toilet, however, required great skill, as Bala realized when he found footprints on his toilet seat during one of Thiru's visits. He had known Thiru for more than 20 years, but never realized he was so talented.

The few calories burned while squatting didn't seem like much, but added up over time. Every little bit of exercise helped, Bala knew. But he was still inclined to avoid the types of everyday exercise his ancestors found necessary. He used elevators instead of stairs, an electric drill instead of a screwdriver, a remote control instead of feet. Like many Americans, he had made it a habit to use drive-thrus, not just at the bank and fast-food restaurants, but also at some yard sales. He wished he could drive through Gigantic Foods too, so he wouldn't have to feel envious of the little children going 'vroom, vroom' inside their car-shaped shopping carts. As it was, he found himself circling the parking lot to find the closest space to the door, sometimes even thinking how lucky the people who parked in the handicapped spaces were.

Looking into the mirror now, marvelling at the size of his stomach, it was clear to him that he needed to eat less and exercise more. He needed to stop having seconds at dinner and be satisfied with firsts and thirds. He needed to not just walk with America, but also run with him. America liked to run, but didn't get enough opportunities, what with so few cats in the neighbourhood and the mailman insisting on using a car.

The front and side views had each revealed a weakness, so Bala decided to check the rear view, using a small mirror from the bathroom. American women, he had noticed, had a thing for men's butts. 'He has such a cute butt,' a middle-aged woman had said on *Oprah*, describing what first attracted her to her husband. It was apparently better to have a cute butt than a great personality. Even so, Bala did not want to have a cute butt. Butts were not supposed to be cute. Butts were functional – they acted as a cushion when you sat, fell or got spanked. And just as importantly, they helped keep your pants up. If God had intended butts to be cute, he would have placed them in front, closer to eye level, as he did with breasts. A cute butt would only bring Bala unnecessary pressure. Whenever he saw a pretty woman, he would face a dilemma: Should he walk forwards or backwards? Walking backwards would make sense, especially since, according to the authors of the how-to book, first impressions were everything. It took just five seconds for a person to decide if they were attracted to a stranger. And by walking backwards, Bala would not only be giving a woman five seconds of butt-watching, he would also be keeping her from five seconds of belly-viewing. But he did not want to look silly, so he was rather relieved when he took a long gaze at his butt and concluded that it did not look cute at all. He dropped his pants just to make sure and quickly pulled them back up. Nothing cute about that, nothing at all. He might even go to the extent of calling it ugly.

Butt ugly. He was pleased to have such a butt, pleased to know that he wouldn't have to walk backwards, except perhaps when leaving a room.

But his delight lasted only a moment, for his eyes wandered upward and he saw what looked like a full moon on a dark night, a light circle surrounded by black. Oh no! He had a bald spot. How could that be? Where did it come from? Appa was balding, it was true, but he was ancient. It was a miracle he had any hair at all. Bala, on the other hand, was far too young to be balding. He didn't even have any kids. Children, according to Appa, were the main reason why a man lost his hair. 'Father without hair loss,' Appa would say, 'is father with good hairpiece.'

Bala ran his fingers across the top of his head, explored the bumpy surface of the moon. It was a fairly big space and it took him a couple of minutes to complete this space exploration. Something must be causing this, something scientific and logical, and he knew what that was: Mr. Ganesan had put a curse on him. He had warned people about gazing at the lecturer's bald head and now he was paying the price. What could he do about this? He couldn't just let people view his scalp. Being bald seemed to be an asset for some men – Michael Jordan and Sean Connery came to mind – but their heads were like oranges, smooth and round. His head was like a pineapple. Perhaps he could grow his hair long in front and comb it all the way back. A comb-over could be quite effective. Appa had employed one for many years, when he still had hair in front. Bala recalled going to Appa's bedroom one night and finding him fast asleep, his hair falling over his face and blowing into the air with every snore. Bala had watched many scary movies in his youth, but had never encountered such a hair-raising scene.

Comb-overs were a family tradition of sorts. Thatha, Appa's Appa, despite being completely bald, had managed to have one too. He covered his entire scalp with two strands of hair that originated from each side of his moustache. It was a sight to behold and Bala had often admired Thatha's ingenuity. But he didn't think he'd be comfortable with a comb-over. Perhaps it would be wiser for him to go with something more natural-looking, something that would be easier to maintain, such as a toupee. He had seen some fine hairpieces on late-night TV. As the infomercials showed, you could do almost anything with a good toupee: swim underwater, climb a mountain, date a supermodel. The 21st century toupee technology was amazing. One company had even created a toupee that would grow along with your bald spot. All you had to do was water it regularly. Though he didn't know then that he might need it, Bala had been very impressed with The Living Toupee. The best part was, he could get one for 'three easy payments of $19.95'. Even if it didn't work well, he would lose less than 60 bucks and could always use The Living Toupee for some other purpose, such as covering his nipples.

But he was only in his late twenties. Did he really need to resign himself to losing his hair? Perhaps he could grow it back. He had heard of bald men applying various products to their heads, such as Rogaine, Instant Hair and Bald-be-gone. Rogaine, in its generic form, was quite affordable; he'd be spending only as much as his neighbour Mrs. Bunch spent on fertilizer, but, unlike her, wouldn't be upset to see a few weeds. Instead of being afraid of hair loss like some men, he would fight this battle to the end, to the very last follicle. It was better to be bold, he told himself, than to be bald.

Perhaps he would also try a pill. These days, you could take a pill for almost anything. Trying to lose weight? Take a pill. Afraid you might get pregnant? Take a pill. Feel like killing your boss? Take a pill. Pills were now considered one of the three major food groups. The other two, of course, were chocolate and ice cream. The most famous pill was Viagra, a potency drug that worked wonders – or so Bala had heard. It had helped many men gain and maintain, at least for a short time, some rather big smiles. Bala was skeptical about some pills, but knew that most were priceless. Without them, people would be walking around in constant anguish: 'Oh, my head. Oh, my back. Oh, my erectile dysfunction.' It was no wonder the early cave-dwelling humans could communicate through only grunts and groans. It took thousands of years for them to learn those three important words: 'Me want pill.' Thankfully, modern doctors were fond of pills. Just last year, Bala had gone to a doctor and the first question she asked was, 'Have you taken any pills?' He considered it a rash diagnosis, because she hadn't taken the time to properly examine his rash. The doctor gave him a prescription, a piece of paper she had scribbled on. He took the paper to a pharmacist, who had spent several years in college learning how to read various types of scribble.

'What does it say?' Bala asked.

'You need lots of pills. Small ones, big ones, white ones, yellow ones, round ones, square ones. It must be quite a rash.'

The pharmacist smiled. Bala knew what he was thinking: 'Now I can buy new shoes for my kids.'

Bala returned home with six bottles of pills. One

kind, he needed to take three times a day, right after meals. Another kind, he needed to take six times a day, on an empty stomach. A third kind, he needed to take once a day, while completely naked. Just figuring out the pill rotation gave him a migraine, which meant he needed a seventh pill. He had no idea what side effects he would experience, because the pill makers, afraid of lawsuits, had warned consumers about every possible reaction: 'Taking this medication could result in sleeplessness, drowsiness, laziness, incontinence, impotence, intelligence, loss of appetite, loss of memory, loss of property. If you're black, it could turn you white. If you're white, it could turn you purple. If you're purple, please see a doctor immediately.'

Even people in good health found themselves taking lots of pills. That's because vitamins and minerals came in pills and so did nutritional supplements. Some bodybuilders spent half their days swallowing pills. And the other half looking in the mirror. Bala was reluctant to take supplements, largely because their long-term effects had not been studied. He was afraid he would wake up one day, a few years later, and find that he had grown a pair of breasts. It was disturbing enough that he had nipples. Of course, if that happened, the supplement makers would be thrilled. They'd find a whole new market in teenage girls. Bala couldn't understand why so many girls and women were interested in making their breasts bigger. He liked small breasts. He had never touched a girl's breasts, but he once touched a woman's – placed his hands right on them while propping up a magazine. It was an issue of *Playboy* that he had bought at the convenience store on one of those nights when *Newsweek* was sold out. Looking at those pictures, he realized that while big breasts filled the pages well, small breasts filled his hands well. Small breasts were attractive and also, he assumed, functional. You could stand on one leg without tipping over, you could run around without jiggling, you could sit in front of a TV without accidentally switching channels.

It mystified Bala why so many women were getting breast implants. It was okay to change your appearance, but not when there were health risks. Bala preferred safe changes, such as the one he had recently made. He had re-grown his moustache, gaining as much hair on his upper lip as he had apparently lost on his head. It wasn't as thick as Appa's – he could never be accused of harbouring a terrorist – but it was thick enough to trap bits of food during lunch and provide a mid-afternoon snack. Not that Bala ever let that happen. He was sure to brush his fingers over his moustache after every meal. He didn't want to be seen walking around with a piece of chicken hanging out of his moustache, especially with so many dogs around. He had shaved his moustache when he came to America, noticing that American men, even the non-religious ones, tended to prefer the choirboy look. Things were quite different in India, where the majority of men sported moustaches. These were no ordinary schoolboy moustaches; these were often prominent, bushy moustaches, the kind that would set you apart, if your neighbour didn't have one too. Bala had grown up watching Tamil movies that featured a moustachioed hero tangling with a moustachioed villain, hoping to win the heart of a moustachioed damsel. But those were old, blurry movies and Bala couldn't be sure if he was just seeing shadows. In newer movies, thankfully, the damsels possessed ultra-smooth upper lips, and in a few well-financed films, even the heroes did. It was only in low-budget movies that directors could not afford special effects.

Indian men were experts at growing and grooming moustaches. A pair of them had even used their moustaches to earn coveted spots in the Guinness Book of World Records. One had lifted 77 pounds of empty gas cylinders with his moustache, setting a record in the increasingly popular sport of moustache weightlifting. Another had grown the longest moustache in the world, a line of hair that spanned 11 feet 11 inches, long enough to reel in a mackerel. Bala was proud of their accomplishments. India had won only a few medals at the Olympic Games, but Bala knew it was only because there were no events involving facial hair.

He looked better with a moustache – he was certain of it – but more importantly, he was comfortable with one. He was a man who was born to be hairy. He came out of his mother's womb with a full head of hair and a wisp or two on his chest. He had grown his first moustache by age 10, which earned him admiration from his friends and a request to appear in the headmaster's office with his birth certificate. It was surprising he was now losing hair on his head, because he had no trouble growing it everywhere else: on his back, on his arms, on his ears. Hair was even growing out of his nose, at such a rapid rate that if he waited a few weeks, he could probably sell it to a wigmaker. But he was afraid that if he didn't clip the hair regularly, it would soon be impossible to breathe. Besides, whenever he looked at men's magazines and read the list of attributes that women found most attractive in men, nose hair was rarely in the Top Ten.

What did make the Top Ten was a man's attire:

women were attracted to well-dressed men, much more
so than to undressed men. This was a major difference
between the sexes. A woman in a thong bikini on the
beach would turn men's heads; a man in a thong would
turn women's stomachs. Bala knew he had to upgrade
his wardrobe to impress women. He owned a few suits
and sports coats, but none was particularly stylish.
They fell into the category of conservative business
wear. Linda, the human resources manager, had once
complimented him, saying, 'You are so with-it, Bala.'
He thanked her, though he wasn't quite sure what it
was he was with. Linda was in her mid-forties and
had lost track of fashion trends, as her polyester suits
indicated. Someone as young as Brooke might consider
him square and unhip, or perhaps, observing him more
closely, round and unhip. He wanted to appear cool to
her and had made it a point to wear loose-fitting Levi
jeans to Gigantic Foods, along with a T-shirt and gold
chain, as he had seen some American musicians do. He
wondered if he should also adopt a hip name, such as
'Master B' or 'Double B'. He wanted to do whatever he
could to impress Brooke and other women.

He was sitting on his couch one evening, sipping a
soft drink, when he had an epiphany, one of those deep
realizations that made him wonder if he was really a
genius, if his head was teeming with unused brain cells.
It was a store-brand soft drink, a ValueTime ginger ale
that cost him 15 cents at Gigantic Foods, about half as
much as a brand-name soft drink like Coke or Sprite.
He was trying to be thrifty, as Appa had taught him to
be. But at this moment, as he was sipping the cheap
soft drink, it dawned on him: This was why he was
still single. This was why women didn't jump all over
him the way they did that Brad Pitt guy. Which woman

would want to be seen with a man who drank cheap soft drinks? A man who drank cheap soft drinks sent a clear message to potential girlfriends: 'On our first date, we'll have a romantic dinner at McDonald's. Don't forget to bring a coupon.'

Bala cringed as he realized he had bought an entire case of cheap soft drinks at Brooke's register. How could he have been so stupid? It was important to project the right image, and a man who drank Coke, Sprite and 7UP exuded sex appeal. It flowed out of his pores. As shown in those TV commercials, when women spotted a man with a real soft drink, they were unable to control themselves. They were drawn to him like children to mud.

The more Bala thought about it, the more he realized that buying a real soft drink was a minimal investment for such a major gain. He used to be proud about saving at least $100 a year by drinking cheap soft drinks, even convincing himself that it tasted as good as the real thing, not realizing he was ruining any chance of getting a date. But now, thankfully, he knew better. Now, armed with a real soft drink or two, he'd be attracting women in droves. He might have to ask them to make appointments. Perhaps he'd need to date several of them on one night. If his social life got too hectic or too expensive, he could always look for ways to reduce his sex appeal. He could always start walking backwards or growing his nose hair. Whatever it took to keep the women at bay.

5

'PABLO FROMRIO IS A MORON, A RAVING LUNATIC. HE went and used the N-word during a speaking engagement. Can you believe it?'

Bala had rarely seen Stewart so angry. 'The N-freaking-word! Can you believe it? So what if he was being heckled – you just don't use the N-word. The F-word and the T-word maybe, but not the N-word.'

Bala wondered what the T-word was. Traitor? Terrorist? Telemarketer?

'I guess he's out for us then,' Mike said. 'We can't use a guy who uses the N-word.'

'That and the fact that he wants three million bucks,' Stewart said. 'Can you believe it? That's more money than we spend in China, almost as much as my wife spends *on* china.'

'His agent says he really did gain weight after the show, almost 50 lbs, and managed to lose most of it recently,' John said. 'They'll be glad to provide us with "before" pictures.'

'I'm sure they would,' Stewart said. 'For three million, they can do a lot of photo buying.'

'Photoshopping,' John said.

'Whatever it's called, they can do a lot of it. Are we really supposed to believe that Pablo managed to double his weight? He wouldn't gain an ounce if you tied him to a bed and pumped Haagen Daz into him.'

'I'd like to tie him to a bed,' John said.

Everyone groaned. 'Sorry, John,' Stewart said, 'but I don't think you can afford him. He's out of your league.'

Mike laughed. 'Yeah, he plays for the other team.'

John rolled his eyes. 'I was just kidding, guys. Pablo isn't exactly my type.'

'Let's get back to business,' Stewart said. 'What about Lori McLules? Should we give her a shot?'

McLules was a former beauty pageant contestant who had represented West Virginia at the 2002 Miss America contest. She had become an internet and tabloid sensation for flubbing one of her questions at the pageant. Asked whom she admired the most and why, she replied, 'Mother Teresa – because she... uh... well... you know... helped India... uh... well... you know... gain independence from... uh... well... you know... Pakistan.'

Widely ridiculed, McLules redeemed herself by appearing on *Oprah* and answering 10 questions correctly. It was an impressive performance for a Miss America contestant, and the audience gave her a standing ovation, overlooking her answers to the other 90 questions.

'I don't think she's been doing much of anything recently,' John said. 'If we're lucky, she has been eating well and gained 200 pounds.'

'200 pounds?' Mike asked. 'The only way for her to gain 200 pounds is to marry Bala.'

'Hey, I'm only 192. No rounding up please.'

'192?' Brian asked. 'Is that with your wallet or without?'

'Without,' Bala said, laughing. 'With my wallet, I'm 225. I can play in the NFL.'

'You're carrying too much money around,' Brian said. 'Haven't you Indians ever heard of a bank? They can be pretty handy.'

'We have banks in India,' Bala said.

'Yeah, we know,' John said, smiling. 'On the side of every river.'

'This is a better kind of bank,' Brian said. 'They'll even give you interest. Just put $1,000 in a savings account and after a year, you can withdraw the interest, go to Wal-Mart and buy yourself a pack of chewing gum.'

'Speaking of money,' Stewart said, 'do you think McLules would do it for 500 grand? That's all we can afford, not one dime more. Check with her agent, John, but we need an answer ASAP. The shipments from China will start arriving in six months. If we don't get some orders by then, we'll have to put them on eBay, along with my Ferrari. That would really tick me off, because I've worked hard in this business and don't want to be seen around town driving just a Mercedes.'

Bala couldn't believe how much money a minor celebrity could make, appearing in an ad or infomercial. $500,000 for a day's work: Who wouldn't want a gig like that? Too bad the job couldn't be outsourced to India. For that kind of dough, they might be able to get a top Bollywood star like Shahrukh Khan to appear in the infomercial, wearing nothing but a pair of Spandex shorts. One flash of his smile and millions of his fans would be buying The Flexerciser – and anything made of Spandex.

Bala tried to sell John and Linda on the idea during lunch one day, but neither of them had even heard of Shahrukh. Bala knew that many celebrities in India were unknown in America, but it still surprised him that there were people on the planet who hadn't heard of Shahrukh, people who weren't in a coma, in a mental institution or in professional wrestling.

Hoping to show his co-workers how popular Shahrukh was, how passionate his fans were, Bala took an issue of *India Dispatch*, a weekly newspaper for Indian-Americans, to work and pointed to a letter to the editor:

Dear Editor,

I am a longtime subscriber to India Dispatch. *It is largely because of you that I'm able to keep up with all the important news from India, particularly the happenings of Bollywood. Like most Indians, I need a regular dose of Bollywood news as much as I need oxygen. Needless to say, I'm also addicted to the movies themselves. In fact, my wife has threatened to divorce me if I don't give up my habit of watching a Bollywood movie every night. I've promised her that I will try my best, however hard it may seem, to survive without her.*

Bollywood is everything to me. That's why I enjoy reading your newspaper. As soon as it arrives in the mail, I grab it, lock myself in the bathroom and turn to the Bollywood section. I read every word, study every picture, trace my finger over every face. I love seeing the pictures of my favourite stars, particularly Shahrukh Khan, who, as you know, is the most popular actor not just in India, but also in New Jersey. So you can imagine my shock and dismay when I opened your latest issue and failed to see a single picture of Shahrukh. At first, I thought I had simply overlooked Shahrukh. I'm so used to seeing his picture that on one occasion, I'm embarrassed to say, I forgot to cut it out. (Thankfully, I was able to retrieve the picture at my local landfill.) Over the last few years, your newspaper has averaged three pictures of Shahrukh per issue. Sometimes he appears in your Bollywood section, sometimes he appears in movie ads, and sometimes he appears in the background of other pictures. For example, you once printed a picture of a new Indian grocery store in New York and, using a magnifying glass, I spotted Shahrukh on two movie posters on the wall. I never realized how much joy a single discovery could bring. But even with the magnifying glass, I couldn't find Shahrukh in your latest issue. My disappointment was so great that for a few days I seriously considered cancelling my subscription.

Then I decided to write this letter, saying to my wife, 'Perhaps the editors don't realize what a grave mistake they've committed.' I should mention that I'm not writing as an ordinary reader, but as the vice-president of the Edison Township, N.J., chapter of the Shahrukh Khan Fan Club. We are affiliated with an extremely powerful organization called NASKA (National Association of Shahrukh Khan Admirers). On behalf of NASKA, I would like to insist that you add a special Shahrukh section to your newspaper to ensure that you never leave him out again. Just remember this: With a single email, I can have twenty busloads of Indians protesting outside your office. Many of us are extremely devoted to Shahrukh. When someone asks us if he's as big as Amitabh, we have only one response: 'Amitabh who?'

Beside the letter, on the adjoining page, was a full-page money-transfer ad featuring a colour picture of Shahrukh, along with a quote: 'Your parents paid for your education. The least you can do is pay for their retirement.'

'Wow,' Linda said. 'He's cute. Very cute.'

'Hey! Hands off!' John said, pulling the paper. 'I want him.'

Bala laughed. 'You and one billion others.'

'Got any of his movies, Bala?' John asked. 'I'd love to see one.'

'I'm sure Sanjay's Rice and Spice Shop has about five hundred, John. I have a few Tamil movies, that's all.'

'Tamil? What country is that?'

Linda shook her head. 'You're so clueless about the world, aren't you, John? Tamil isn't a country. It's a religion. Just like Hindi.'

'Whom do Tamils worship?'

'We worship Rajinikanth. He's an actor.'

'Really?' Linda asked. 'Is he as cute as Share Rook Can?'

'Don't ask me. I'm not a woman. My mother's crazy about him though. She has seen every one of his movies at least a dozen times. When I was growing up, she watched so many movies on TV, she didn't have much time to cook. Finally, my father put his foot down.'

'What did he do – turn the TV off?' Linda asked.

'No, he moved it to the kitchen. When I left India, we had TVs in three rooms – much to my father's dismay – and sometimes there was a different Rajinikanth movie on each of them. My mother wasn't the only Rajinikanth fan, you know.'

'Really?' Linda asked. 'Was your sister into him too?'

'My sister, me, my grandmother, the servant girl, the woman who ironed our clothes, and the squirrels that peeked through the kitchen window.'

'Rage Knee Cat must be a god,' Linda said. 'I need to google him.'

'He *is* a god,' Bala said. 'Some people have built

shrines for him. And others have done it for Shahrukh. Some fans are so poor that whenever they buy a movie ticket, they have to skip a meal. I saw one being interviewed on TV. "I'm hungry for food," she said, "but not as much as I'm hungry for Shahrukh.'"

'That's crazy,' John said. 'Although I have to say, Shahrukh does look delectable.'

'Tasty,' Linda added.

'Oh please,' Bala said, laughing. 'You two are just as crazy.'

He made a mental note to invite them to his place to watch a Bollywood movie. He could rent a DVD with English subtitles, so he wouldn't have to translate. His Hindi wasn't very good anyway. He had taken it as a third language in school, but it had eventually become a fourth language, behind English, Tamil and SMS. He and his college friends had often used the short messaging system (or texting) to chat on cell phones or the Internet. With one hand holding a pole on the bus or a shoulder on a two-wheeler, they could tap out messages with the other.

'R u cmng 4 crkt mtch?'

'No, wtchng Rjni mvie.'

'Crkt bttr thn Rjni.'

'Thts blsht.'

They liked SMS because there were no rules, no one enforcing the grammar or punctuation. But it was easy to be misunderstood, as they realized when Thiru got a message from a female friend in college: 'U gv me lc.'

'I give her luck. Is that what she's saying?'

'No, Thiru,' Gopal said. 'She is saying that you gave her lice. What you were doing with her?'

As it turned out, the classmate had merely forgotten her tiffin: 'You give me lunch.'

Despite its shortcomings, sms was a good third language. But nowadays Bala wished his third language had been Chinese, more specifically Mandarin. That would have made it easier to communicate with Li Chao, the chief engineer at the factory. While all the design work and testing was done in Harrisburg, all the manufacturing was done in Shanghai. After the final drawings and specs had been sent to the factory, Bala still needed to spend weeks making sure everything was clear. To ease communication, the company had hired an engineer named Ming Chao, whose English was impeccable. But that only made things worse, as Ming Chao and Li Chao clashed almost every week.

'We used to have just one Chao,' Stewart said. 'Now we have Chaos.'

Ming Chao was young and confident, a know-it-all. Li Chao was middle-aged and circumspect: he didn't want to jump to conclusions or proceed without making sure he was doing the right thing. He was the driver who would get a green light, yet look both ways to make sure no one was coming. Ming Chao was the driver honking behind him.

'He no good,' Li Chao complained to Bala one day. 'He want make mistake. Company lose money.'

'What did he do now?'

'Now? He home now. Me not know what he do.'

'No, I mean, what did he do this time?'

'This time? This time, he home. You no hear?'

'No, I mean, what did he do the other time?'

'Other time? Other time when?'

At times like this, Bala felt like shouting into the phone. But he took a deep breath and reminded himself of Rajini's advice in *Padayappa*: '*Kattapaadu vennum ippadi kathakoodathu*. (Self-control is needed. You can't scream.)'

Still, he couldn't help getting a little frustrated. It was no wonder he was losing hair. At this rate, he would be as bald as a potato before The Flexerciser hit the market. Thankfully, he had started using Rogaine, applying it morning and night. It had been just a week, but he had already noticed a few new hairs. Four around his right nipple, two around his left. None, unfortunately, on his head, though he couldn't be sure. It was hard to tell exactly what was happening on top of his head, because his eyes were halfway down the other side. The two-mirror method didn't work that well, didn't permit a thorough examination, so he decided to try a more modern way. He sat on a chair, looked downward, and held his digital camera over his head. After snapping a dozen pictures, he downloaded them onto his laptop computer and used the zoom feature to scan the surface of the moon. There was no new life there, as far as he could tell. His chest was more fertile and he was beginning to understand why: it was harder for hair to grow upward, against the force of gravity, than to pop out sideways and downward. This theory would explain what was happening in his nose. Perhaps if he hung upside down for several hours every day, his hair would grow in all the right places. He made a note of the upside-down strategy in his computer, calling it 'Plan Z'.

He knew he had to be patient. His self-improvement plan might take a few weeks, or even months, to produce results. He had not lost any weight yet, despite being on a diet for almost ten days. Every time he saw something good to eat – doughnuts, cake, fried chicken – he reminded himself he was on a DIET, which, in his case, stood for 'Darn, I'm eating this.'

It was hard to reduce calories, especially since he was also trying to improve his image by drinking lots of real soft drinks. Coke was his favourite – he didn't care for the diet drinks – and each can added 150 calories to his daily intake. He had bought three cases of Coke, seventy-two cans in all, at Gigantic Foods and smiled at Brooke as he placed them on the conveyor belt. It was amazing how much confidence Coke had already given him, even before taking a single sip.

Brooke smiled back and asked, 'How are you today?'

'Fine, thank you. How are you?'

'Pretty good, especially since my shift's about to end.'

He was pleased that she had asked him a question that wasn't part of her job requirement, a question other than 'Paper or plastic?' Their relationship had progressed to a new level, all because he had been smart enough to buy Coke.

It was only on the drive home that he realized what an opportunity he had missed. Her shift was ending – he could have asked her if she'd like to grab a bite somewhere. Isn't that what an American man would have done? But it took courage to ask a woman out, unless you knew her well. Bala didn't have that kind of courage, but he was confident that if he kept buying Coke, kept drinking it, it was only a matter of time before Brooke asked him out.

Still, he didn't want to depend completely on soft drinks, which reminded him of his social life: bubbly one moment, flat the next. He consulted the how-to book to see if there was anything else he could do to show Brooke he liked her. On Page 72, in the middle of a chapter called 'Be Persistent', he found an option he hadn't seriously considered. 'Women love receiving flowers and not just on Valentine's Day,' the authors wrote. 'Just remember: you have nothing to lose, except $69.99.' He had never sent flowers to a woman before, partly because he remembered Linda's reaction when she received a dozen roses from her Mexican boyfriend, Miguel. She read the attached card and started crying. The only time Bala had shed so many tears, India had lost to Australia in the World Cup.

Women didn't always appreciate flowers, but at least the men didn't have to be around to see the reaction. It was usually a safe way of endearing yourself to a woman. Bala would still have to stick his neck out, but only as far as the flower shop. He wished he knew Brooke's last name – was it Smith or Brown or Jones? What if there was another Brooke at Gigantic Foods? It was important to be specific, otherwise Bala might end up courting the elderly woman in the bakery department.

He visited Will's Flower Shop on McMullen Street, just two blocks from his house, and selected an arrangement of carnations for $29.99.

'Who is it going to?' the bearded man asked.

'A clerk at Gigantic Foods. I don't know her last name, but you can just write "Brooke, the clerk with blonde hair and pink lipstick."'

'Works for me. Who is it from?'

'Bala, your favourite customer.'

'How do you spell that?'

'Actually, you can just write B-I-L-L.'

'Bill?'

'Yes, I'm from India. Bill is Bala in India.'

'Really? That's very interesting. My name is Will. What would I be in India?'

'Wala. Or more precisely Flower-wala.'

Bala spent a minute explaining what 'wala' or 'wallah' meant in India. He missed all the wallahs – the vegetable-wallah, the milk-wallah, the coconut-wallah. There were so many vendors on the streets of Chennai, you couldn't turn a corner without running into one of them. They often brought their goods right past people's homes, yelling 'Vegetables!' or 'Fish!' or 'Nuts!' They were the unsung heroes of the economy, contributing greatly to India's productivity, because with all their shouting, no one could take a nap. But Bala loved that aspect of India – being able to not only buy things on the street, but also bargain with the vendors. When he came to America, he was pleased to discover that he could still buy things on the street and bargain with the sellers, as long as he drove around and looked for signs that said 'Yard sale'. He enjoyed this form of discount shopping, because it was so unpredictable. You never knew what you might find at a yard sale: a microwave, a colour TV, a used toilet seat. Bala saw a used toilet seat at one yard sale and wondered who would buy such a thing. But as he stood there, a woman actually bought it. She snapped it right up. Didn't even ask who sat on it. He would have. But then he felt the urge to ask a lot of questions at yard sales: In which century did you buy it? Was it ever used by the dog? How many times did the baby throw up on it?

At some yard sales, people even gave away things for free. One Saturday, Bala found an old Abba record with a $1 price tag. He wondered if it was a collector's item. Noticing his interest, the greying man running the yard sale said, 'Go ahead and take that, if you like it.' Bala tried to offer him some money, but the man said, 'Take it. It's yours. I don't need no "Money, Money".' Bala shrugged and said, 'Okay, if you insist... Thank you for the music.' He had hoped to bargain with the man. He could have brought the price down to 75 cents and felt good about saving 25 cents. Now he wondered if he was taking home a piece of junk.

Americans were just no good at bargaining. Many of them accepted the first offer they got. There were exceptions, of course. Some were business-minded and knew what they were doing. A few had even worked their way up the ladder and were now professional yard-sellers. They made enough money on weekends to take the week off. These were the people who were selling all kinds of fitness equipment, but looked like they'd never had a minute of exercise in their lives. These were the people who had a safe for their money, just in case some desperate robber decided to hold up a yard sale. These were the people who never ran out of merchandise, because they kept stocking their garage with stuff from other yard sales. Bala liked these people because they not only bargained skillfully with him, some of them even accepted Visa and MasterCard.

He had twenty-seven credit cards to his name, including a platinum card from Citibank, a gold card from Chase Manhattan and an aluminum card from Goodwill. Companies were always sending him offers and he was always accepting them, just in case. At first, he felt good about receiving all these offers, imagining his stellar reputation in the financial world, but that was before a new credit card arrived in the mail for America. It was from a store in Capital City Mall called Pet Electronics. Bala had visited the store to see the latest gadgets for pets. He had almost bought America an iDog®, so they could both enjoy music while jogging. He also liked the Dogmatick®, a device that fit on a dog's collar and growled whenever it detected a tick. But like the iDog®, it was a little pricey. As Bala was leaving the store, a salesman convinced him to fill out a survey, saying he had a chance to win a Dogital Watch®. Bala liked the idea of giving America a watch that emitted a 'woof' every hour and a 'meow' at feeding times. He completed the survey quickly, putting both his and America's name in the appropriate spaces. Three weeks later, the credit card arrived in the name of America Balasubramaniam. Bala wondered if he should help America use it. Perhaps it was wise, in the 21st century, for dogs to develop credit histories of their own. But was it morally wrong to get your pet in debt? It was true that so many Americans were in debt and America itself was in debt. But did it make sense for America to do what America did? These were questions that Bala pondered. He couldn't help comparing the two Americas. One was more likely to lick its enemies, but less likely to lick itself. One was more likely to sleep around the clock, but less likely to sleep around. One was more likely to harm the environment, but less likely to harm the mailman.

Bala was glad America had a credit card, but he really didn't need the extra credit. With his twenty-seven cards, he had accumulated enough credit to buy a jumbo jet. It would offer direct flights from Harrisburg to Chennai, serve wine with every meal, and be called, of course, Indian Airwines. Passengers would be given three meal choices: very spicy, super spicy and deadly spicy. The in-flight entertainment would be a movie marathon: The Best of Rajinikanth. Anyone who could name twenty-five Rajini movies would be moved to First Class. Anyone who could name fifty would be moved to the cockpit.

Bala would be able to fly home monthly and his

parents would finally get to see America. He had sent them pictures, but until they actually experienced America firsthand, they wouldn't be able to appreciate what a great dog he was. But did Bala really want to see his parents that often? Probably not, especially Appa, who would just keep telling him what a waste the airplane was. 'Travelling by train is better and cheaper than any other mode of transportation,' Appa was fond of saying, speaking with so much conviction that Bala, as a child, had believed there were tracks across the ocean. To Appa, a train trip was an experience to be savoured. He tried to get his children to appreciate the beautiful scenery: the rice fields, the coconut groves, the rivers and streams. Bala had learned to appreciate the streams, particularly the stream of vendors calling out 'Samosa!' and 'Vadai!' They flowed down the aisle, carrying their food trays aloft, filling each cabin with a smell so tantalizing, even Appa couldn't resist reaching for his wallet. Eating during a train journey was a good way to pass time, but Bala found it hard to maintain a balance, to eat just enough that he didn't have to visit the toilet, where it was even harder to maintain a balance.

At least once a year during his secondary school and college days, Bala had taken the Pearl City Express to visit Uncle and Aunty Balakrishnan and their three children, Hari, Shiva and Vani. The train left Egmore Station at 6:30 p.m. and arrived in Thoothukudi at 6:30 the next morning. Bala enjoyed talking to other passengers, learning everything about them, where they worked, how many children they had, what their favourite Rajini movie was. Just one question could spark a long conversation. Older people were prone to ramble, but Bala didn't mind at all, for while they were sharing their stories, they also shared their food. The conversations helped pass time; the evening disappeared in a matter of minutes and then it was time to pull up the sleepers and turn in for the night. Bala always took the top berth. He felt safer up there. If a bridge collapsed and the train fell into a river, the water might not reach him. He knew that other passengers would find his fear irrational, but *they* didn't know who was designing the bridges.

Bala would spend a whole week in Thoothukudi, but with all the activities Hari and Shiva involved him in – cricket, badminton, kabaddi – it was over before he even had a chance to see all the servants. He also saw little of Vani, who tended to keep to herself, reading books in her room, watching serials on TV or doing whatever it was girls did. She made her appearances mostly at mealtimes and even then, didn't sit with her twin brothers or father, but helped the cook serve them. As each chapatti or dosa came off the pan, she would bring it to the dining table and drop it on the first plate that looked half-empty, ignoring any objection that wasn't expressed at the decibel level of a jumbo jet. She hardly smiled, but at least when she made her quick turn at the table, her long plaited hair swung from side to side like the tail of a happy dog. It was the type of prompt service Bala missed when he came to America. A few Indian restaurants did give him 'service with a smile,' but others were split evenly between 'service with no smile' and 'smile with no service'. At one restaurant, Bombay Palace, he was treated to the 'no smile, no service' approach. He did see the waiters smile on occasion, but only when picking up tips.

He was glad Brooke had smiled at him. It didn't cost anything to smile and Brooke had the type of smile that four out of five dentists wouldn't change. Bala wished he could have been standing in the store to see her smile when she received the flowers. Instead, he went to the store the next day to buy another case of Coke, hoping it would give him the courage to introduce himself to her. As he placed the case on the conveyor belt, he smiled and said, 'How are you?'

She smiled back. 'Pretty good, thank you. How are you?'

'Fine.' He paused, took a deep breath. 'I'm Bill, by the way.'

'I'm Jennifer.'

Jennifer? He was stunned, perplexed. As she swiped his credit card, he pulled his eyes off her face long enough to read the entire tag on her shirt, just above her left breast. It said:

'BROOKE BOND. Red Label Tea. Now available at Gigantic.'

6

IT WAS HIS FAULT, REALLY. IF HE HAD READ HER NAME IN full, he would have realized it wasn't her name at all. But he hadn't expected the store to advertise on her chest, even if it was a good way to reach male customers. Advertising was going too far these days. Some Americans now found themselves living in the City of Cisco, watching football in PlayStation Park, sunbathing at eBay Beach, getting treatment at Dr. Pepper Hospital and worshipping at St. Pauli Girl Cathedral. A few companies and groups were even paying people to tattoo ads on their bodies. Bala had spotted a man walking shirtless on the street with 'Goodyear' tattooed across his spare tyre. He had also seen a woman with 'Got Milk?' tattooed above her breasts, which caused him to swear off dairy products for a month. Other companies were rewarding parents who named their children after particular products, paying them enough to send Vaseline and Listerine to college. The most popular girls' names were Fanta, Carnation and Nivea. The most popular boys' names were Ford, Armani and Colgate. Bala wondered what would happen if Colgate took a liking to Nivea. Would she brush him off? Would he rub her the wrong way? Or would they unite and produce offspring with perfect teeth and skin?

Even ordinary people were advertising in strange ways. Bala was driving to work one morning when a bumper sticker on a red Porsche caught his eye. It read: 'Honk if you want me.' Bala immediately honked, because he had never seen such an attractive car. He wanted it, even if he couldn't afford it. But the man in the car just glared at Bala. He didn't look pleased at all.

Perhaps the man was tired of people honking at him. Bala realized that the space on his bumper was quite valuable – it could be used to attract attention, preferably from the opposite sex. He could place several stickers on his bumper with messages such as: 'Honk if you want the driver and you're female,' 'Honk if you think Indian accents are sexy,' 'Honk if you can pronounce Balasubramaniam.' But what would happen after a woman honked? Would he pull over and try to meet her? What if she was five inches taller than him? What if she was ten inches wider than him? What if she had been divorced four times and widowed twice, with both husbands dying under mysterious circumstances? The more he thought about it, the more he realized how risky drive-by dating could be.

Thankfully, there were many other ways to meet women, as the how-to book showed. He was determined to try several methods. He didn't want to put all his eggs in one basket, because if they happened to hatch at the same time, he might end up with dozens of chicks fighting over him. It was smarter to keep them separate.

The important thing, the book said, was to get involved in activities where he was likely to meet women. Joining a social club or community group was a good way to do this. Bala looked in the lifestyle section of the *Patriot-News* and found a list of groups that welcomed new members. He quickly ruled out some of them, including the Anger Management Group (he didn't want to meet angry women), the Tobacco Dependence Recovery Group (he didn't want to meet jittery women) and the Knitting and Crochet Club (he didn't want to meet women with sharp objects).

The Harrisburg Area Bikers Club looked promising. 'Join us at 9 a.m. next Saturday on City Island for our 10K Sociable Fun Ride along the Susquehanna River, followed by brunch at Melissa's Restaurant,' the listing said. 'Beginner and intermediate bikers welcome.' Bala had owned a bicycle in Chennai and always enjoyed riding it. The Bikers Club would enable him to get some much-needed exercise while meeting single women – women who were bound to be in great shape. He needed to buy a good bike first. He shopped around and got lucky on his fifth stop, finding one for only $60 at a yard sale. It had everything he was looking for: two wheels, a seat and a handlebar. The seller, a dark-haired man in his thirties, said the bike was seven years old, but it looked much newer. Its red paint still gleamed, the tyres had a lot of tread left, and the bell seemed to be sufficiently grating to the ear. Bala bargained the price down to $45 and even got the man to toss a rusty bicycle pump into the deal. Bala hadn't yet bought any tall buildings or casinos, but it was clear to him that he possessed the type of negotiating skills Donald Trump would envy.

As Bala left the yard sale, the man said, 'Sorry I don't have a helmet to sell you.' Bala chuckled. He wondered if it was a joke. Surely this bicycle didn't go fast enough to require a helmet. Perhaps American bikes were designed to go faster than Indian ones. His bike did look more aerodynamic, with no carrier in the back and a seat so narrow, he would have to get his butt cheeks to take turns. He would also need to remember to use his brakes to stay at a safe speed. When he started riding in Chennai, he used his brakes constantly on the busy roads. People were often getting in the way – and so were some reckless animals. They thought they owned the road, just because they were on motorbikes. Over time, he learnt to conserve his brakes by reacting quickly and dodging people. But he wasn't always successful and had a heated argument with one young woman, who just couldn't be pacified, even after Bala suggested politely that her sari looked better with the extra print.

Eager to see if his riding skills were still sharp, he awoke early that Saturday morning to prepare for the fun ride. He wore a pair of loose sweatpants and a green T-shirt. He had a breakfast of cornflakes and orange juice, then did some warm-up exercises, including twenty sit-ups and just as many sit-downs. He packed his refreshments for the ride, a banana and two cans of Coke. He hung them from his handlebar using a plastic grocery bag.

He lived only two miles from the City Island parking lot near Walnut Street Bridge, where the group was to meet, but much of the trip was uphill and by the time he got there, he was exhausted. He felt like drinking a Coke, but decided to wait until all the bikers were there. Why waste a brand-name soft drink on just thirst? The Sociable Fun Ride group had not arrived yet, but another group of riders was assembling at the far end of the lot. They looked like professionals, wearing helmets, Lycra shorts, and gloves. Their bikes looked new and sleek and fast. Were they taking part in some kind of race? Was this the first stage of the Tour de Pennsylvania? Bala was glad his group was late – it would give him a chance to watch the beginning of this race. He had never seen a bike race, except on TV. He once caught highlights of the Tour de France and admired the winner, an American cyclist with an apt name: Lance Legstrong.

One of the men, wearing black shorts and a yellow jersey, rode up to him and smiled. 'Joining us?'

'No. I'm not that fast.'

'Neither are we.'

'That's okay. I'm taking part in another ride.'

'Really? What ride is that?'

'The Sociable Fun Ride.'

The man chuckled. 'That's us! Don't we look sociable enough?'

His name was Curtis and he was the leader of the group. He introduced Bala to some of the other riders, including a woman named Karen who made his eyes pop. She had the type of body every man desired: bulging biceps, broad shoulders, muscular legs. Bala wished he could have her body. Then he'd really be able to impress other women. There were six women in all, among a group of 21, and Bala met four of them. The most attractive was a curvaceous brunette named Sandra. Bala wished he could have her body. But it was a fleeting thought, for he knew it was important to get to know her character, her personality. It was enjoyable to admire a woman's body, but far more rewarding to appreciate her on a deeper level. He had learnt this lesson at Saraswathi Higher Secondary School (SHSS) in Chennai: a girl in his class named Priya Matthew had won his affection, though she was hardly a head-turning beauty. It was her self-assurance and sense of humour that captivated him. She was determined to become a professional cartoonist and often entertained him with caricatures of the teachers. When Mr. Venkatesh, the mathematics teacher, pinched Bala's arm mercilessly for arriving late to class, Priya depicted the teacher as Shylock, trying to extract a pound of flesh. Her cartoon was gleefully passed around the class, before ending up on Bala's bedroom wall. From then on, students exchanged comments such as 'Shylock is quite a character' and 'Shylock is mean and nasty,' pleasing Mrs. Mutthiah, the literature teacher, who believed that they, like her, had fallen under the spell of Shakespeare. Bala gave his friend a nickname that she would grow to love: Shakespriya.

Priya's aspiration to become something other than a doctor or engineer inspired Bala, deepened his desire to become a film director, motivated him to get serious and make a list of actresses who would appear in his first movie.

When he eventually decided to apply to engineering college, Priya tried in vain to dissuade him. 'Haven't you heard the saying "Be all that you can be"?' she asked.

'Yes, but I've also heard my father's saying: "B.E. is all that you can be."'

'Your father already has *his* B.E. He doesn't need to get one through you. You have to follow your own goals, your own dreams. You've got only one life, you know.'

'Only one life? You poor Christians. You don't believe in reincarnation. How sad!'

He had developed a great fondness for her and even put his arm around her now and then, but they remained just friends. A closer relationship didn't seem practical, given their dissimilar backgrounds. His family was Tamil; hers was Malayali. His liked Rajinikanth; hers preferred Mammooty. His was resolutely vegetarian; hers had scared all the squirrels away.

There was something about Sandra that reminded him of Priya. Perhaps it was her curly hair, swirling down from her helmet, or maybe it was her brownish skin, almost as dark as his. He wondered if that was her natural complexion or if she had grilled herself in the sun, as so many Americans did. He didn't eat steaks, but she made him think of them: a 'rare' woman who was also 'well-done'. He was glad he wasn't the only dark-skinned person there; it was awkward enough that he was the only one in sweatpants, the only one who wasn't wearing a helmet, the only one who didn't appear to have a corporate sponsor.

As the bikers got ready to go, Bala set a goal for himself: to ride alongside Sandra and strike up a conversation. Perhaps he would share some biking tips with her, help her go faster. By the time they reached the restaurant, they would be chatting like old friends. It seemed like a good plan, but only until the ride began, only until she left him in another area code. He pushed the pedals with all his strength, but just couldn't keep up with her. She was in such great shape that all he could do was look admiringly at her from behind and say to himself, 'Nice shape!'

This was supposed to be a 'fun ride', but most of the others had left him behind too. He was beating only two riders: a middle-aged man with a brace around his knee and a pregnant woman. He was determined not to let them both pass him. Otherwise he wouldn't be able to face everyone at the restaurant. He'd just have to walk back home after dumping his bike in the river.

He passed a bench on Front Street, where two young women were sitting, and sped up to impress them. But he couldn't maintain the pace for more than a minute. He heard a whirling sound behind him and glanced back. The pregnant woman was catching up to him, only a bike length behind. He was straining to stay ahead of her, pumping his legs harder than ever before, the Coke cans clanging against the handlebar. He tried switching gears, but that made no difference. Perhaps his gear system was defective. Did yard sales have a return policy?

Just before turning off Front Street, he glanced back again and saw the woman drinking from a sport bottle. She looked relaxed, breathing comfortably, like she was at the beach, reading a Grisham novel. Some of the other riders were drinking from sport bottles too. What was in them? Water? Gatorade? Performance-enhancing drugs?

Whatever it was, it seemed to be giving them plenty of energy. Perhaps he needed to re-energize himself too. He reached into the grocery bag and pulled out a Coke. He tried to open the can with one hand, using his teeth as a lever. But he couldn't pull the tab up – it was too close to the lid – and he had to take his other hand off the handlebar. His bike swerved to the curb and in that instant, as he tried to perform this circus maneuver, the pregnant woman passed him. She zipped by him like an Olympic rider seizing an opportunity. He swore and pulled the tab up. His bike hit the curb and Coke splattered onto his face. 'Clumsy idiot!' he said to himself.

Luckily, he was able to put his foot down and prevent an embarrassing fall. He straightened the bike and resumed pedaling, just as the middle-aged man passed him too. He sipped the Coke and felt refreshed. It gave him enough energy to pedal a little faster and within five minutes he caught up to the pregnant woman, who had fallen behind the middle-aged man. She looked tense, breathing heavily, like she was about to go into labor. Moments before they reached the restaurant, with a last determined push, he edged past her. He felt ecstatic, a wave of euphoria splashing over him. He hadn't ridden a bike in years and yet had managed to finish in the Top Twenty.

The middle-aged man was locking his bike when Bala arrived.

'Nice ride!' Bala said.

'Yes, I really enjoyed that. My leg hardly hurt at all.'

Bala looked down and was stunned. The man wasn't just wearing a knee brace, he had an artificial leg coming out of it. Bala had lost to a one-legged man. He looked at the man's bike, just to make sure it didn't have a motor of some sort. Perhaps it was jet-propelled. But everything looked normal, even the pedals. He felt like screaming at the man: 'What's wrong with you? Don't you know that you're supposed to be disabled?' It was crazy what many disabled people were doing these days – accomplishing so much in their lives and making able-bodied people look like total bums. Some were simply amazing. Bala had heard of a blind man who had learned to play golf, a paraplegic woman who had learned to skydive, and a New York cabdriver with no hands who had learned to show other drivers his middle toe.

Bala felt better when he entered the restaurant. A seat facing Sandra was empty and, with a few quick steps, he beat the pregnant woman to it. The bikers were sitting at two adjacent tables, taking up almost half the space in the restaurant. Bala felt like he was at a FlexIt management meeting, except there were six conversations going on at once and no one was eating doughnuts. They were having pancakes, eggs, home fries, bacon and sausage. Bala helped himself to some pancakes and eggs. Someone passed him a platter of sausage and he put three links on his plate. He could always throw it up later. He liked to do that – bring something home and throw it in the air for America to catch.

'How did you like the ride, Bill?' Curtis asked from the end of the table.

'Too short,' Bala said. 'Another 20 miles and I would have passed all of you.'

Sandra smiled. 'Another 20 miles and I would have passed *out.*'

Bala laughed, louder than anyone else. She had a good sense of humour, yet another similarity to Priya. Wouldn't it be amazing if *her* family liked Mammooty too?

'That wasn't supposed to be a race,' said Karen, the muscle-bound woman. 'But I won anyway. What's the prize?'

'An extra piece of bacon,' Curtis said, handing her the platter.

'Oh good!' she said. 'My husband expects me to bring home the bacon.' She nudged the skinny man next to her.

'I wish mine would,' Sandra said. 'Then I'd have something to put on my résumé – other than underwear-folding.'

Everyone laughed, louder than Bala. What he really wanted to do was scream. She was married! Taken! Folding some guy's underwear!

Why wasn't she wearing a ring? Weren't married people supposed to wear rings? Wasn't that the law in America? He had grown accustomed to looking for a ring. Every time he saw a potential mate, his eyes automatically drifted to her ring finger. It was amazing how that worked – how you could suddenly notice things you hadn't noticed before. After Bala bought his Toyota Corolla, he started seeing them everywhere: on the roads, in parking lots, even in movies. Whenever he pulled up next to another Corolla at a traffic light, he would look at the other driver and wonder what else they had in common. But when the other driver looked at him, he would immediately look away. It was the polite thing to do. After you had done some staring, you had to give the other person a chance to do the same.

When breakfast was over, Bala discreetly wrapped the sausage links in a napkin, so he could put them in the grocery bag, next to the Coke and banana. As he was leaving, he passed the pregnant woman unlocking her bike and tried to be friendly.

'When are you expecting?'

She glared at him, the type of withering look that made him wish the earth would open up and swallow him alive.

'Expecting what?'

'Uh... expecting to get to the bridge. Does it take longer going back?'

Her expression softened. 'No, it's about the same, maybe a tenth of a mile longer. I'll ride with you if you'd like.'

He knew he hadn't covered up his faux pas convincingly. Perhaps she was in a forgiving mood or perhaps she wanted to believe she didn't really look pregnant. Whatever the case, he felt like an idiot, too stupid to realize that in this age of widespread obesity – when he himself looked like he was eating for two – a woman was not pregnant until she said she was. And even then, only a few men would comment on her size, the type of men who would also stick their hands in an alligator tank.

He wished he hadn't said anything to her, but part of him also felt better that it wasn't a pregnant woman who had almost beaten him – it was merely an overweight one. But how had it gotten this bad? How had he allowed himself to get so out-of-shape that even overweight women were giving him a challenge? Just six years ago, before coming to America, he had considered himself athletic. He was such a good cricket player that his cousin Hari had nicknamed him 'Nine-dulkar', saying he was just a notch below the great Indian batsman Tendulkar. If Hari saw him today, he'd surely give him another nickname: 'One-dulkar'.

7

BALA NEEDED TO GET INTO SHAPE, NEEDED TO AT LEAST ATTAIN a four or five on the Dulkar Scale. But until then, it was wise to meet women through activities that didn't require physical exertion. He looked at the *Patriot-News* listings again and jotted three possibilities: a Scrabble club, book discussion group and golf league. He had never played golf before, but how hard could it be? All he had to do was walk around, hitting a ball into a hole, while his caddy carried his equipment. If necessary, he could always take a golf course and learn the fundamentals of the game. There were many golf courses in the area, according to the phone book. But golf was an expensive game and, with all that open space, there was a high risk of being struck by lightning. He had heard somewhere – was it on *SportsCenter*? – that a golfer was 10,000 times more likely to be struck by lightning than a Scrabble player. Scrabble players, in general, had little reason to strike golfers.

Scrabble was safer and cheaper than golf, but on the downside, it was often more physically challenging. You had to put your hand in a bag and pick letters. You had to put them on a rack and shield them from roving eyes. When it was your turn, you had to somehow make a word – a real word, not one of those sms words. And then you had to endure one of the most exhausting aspects of the game: waiting for your opponents to play.

Considering everything, Bala decided that the book discussion was his best bet. It seemed like something attractive women would do – sit around and discuss books. They might even talk about the author, how pretty she looked in the picture on the book jacket, how terribly unfortunate that her lipstick clashed with her blouse.

Bala called the number in the listing and spoke to a woman named Helen, who had a sweet voice. 'We're always looking for new members,' she said. 'We need to liven up our discussions.' The group met the last Friday of every month in the coffee shop at Ebby's Independent Bookstore. At the next meeting, they would be discussing the novel *The Namesake*.

'It's a good book,' Helen said. 'You've probably heard of the author: Jumper La Hairy. She's won the Pulitzer Prize.'

Bala was glad he wouldn't need to read the book. He had just seen the movie. He tried to persuade Thiru, who had also seen the movie, to drive up and attend the book discussion with him. But Thiru didn't seem interested in meeting women, though he was the same age as Bala – hurtling toward 30. When Bala spoke of marriage, Thiru only recited common jokes about it: 'First comes the engagement ring. Then comes the wedding ring. Then comes the suffering.' He also thought Bala was fooling himself, believing he could get away with marrying a white woman. 'Your parents will kill you!' he said. 'They will set your kundi on fire! And if they find out I assisted you, they will castigrate me.'

'I think you mean "castigate",' Bala said.

'Yes, castigate. They will castigate me and I won't be able to have children.'

If Bala's parents could not come to America to kill him, they would follow a strategy that had been perfected by other Indian parents, Thiru said. First, they would threaten to disown Bala. 'You are not our son anymore,' Appa would say. 'From now on, you are the idiot formerly known as our son.'

If that didn't work, one of them, probably Appa, would suddenly fall deathly ill. 'For your father's sake, you must cancel the wedding,' Amma would say. 'The doctor says that any type of stress, any kind of worry, will cause him to have a heart attack, kidney failure, maybe even AIDS.'

If that didn't work, one of them, probably Amma, would threaten to commit suicide. 'I would rather die than see my son bring shame upon my family,' she would say. 'Please do not come for my cremation. Your father will take care of everything – if he recovers from his illnesses.'

Bala conceded that his parents would probably not welcome a white daughter-in-law with open arms. But he believed they'd eventually come around, they'd eventually realize that opposing their son's wishes was like putting a bullock cart in front of a freight train. Thiru insisted they'd never fully accept her. They wouldn't treat her like a normal daughter-in-law – they wouldn't let her wait on them hand and foot.

'Oh, how sad!' Bala said. 'They will have to get coffee for themselves.'

'*You* will have to get coffee for yourself, too,' Thiru said, laughing. 'American women won't treat you like a prince. Just ask my boss, Deepak. He was married to an American for three years and you won't believe it – she wanted him to do the laundry sometimes. Can you imagine?' Thiru scrunched his face like it was the most revolting thing he had heard.

'Laundry is no big deal,' Bala said. He had, after all, done his own laundry hundreds of times, even separating the clothes in the washer: whites on the bottom, colours on top.

But there was a lot more to consider when marrying an American woman, Thiru said. If Bala wore a dhoti or lungi at home, his wife may laugh and say, 'Did you run out of clothes again? Why are you wearing our bed sheet?' If she found him eating rice with his fingers, she may hand him a fork and say, 'Here's a new invention you may find useful.' And if he put too much chilli powder in the chicken curry, he may find himself in court, accused of spousal abuse. 'Oh my God! Were you trying to kill me?' his wife may yell. 'Or were you just trying to make sure the chicken was dead?'

Bala knew there'd be cultural differences to contend with, but as long as his wife was open-minded, as long as she appreciated other cultures, they'd be able to bridge the differences. Besides, American women were not all of one kind – and neither were Indian women. He just needed to find a good woman, preferably one who didn't mind having her tongue burned now and then.

He was looking forward to meeting women at the book discussion. Such women were probably open-minded, having read about other cultures in books. He was particularly eager to get to know Helen, who sounded so friendly on the phone. He pictured her with blond hair and blue eyes, dimples gracing her cheeks. It was a fairly accurate picture, as he discovered when he arrived at the bookstore that Friday evening: she had blond hair and blue eyes, wrinkles gracing her cheeks. There were six women seated around a table and Helen, in her fifties, was by far the youngest.

'It's nice to have a man for a change,' she said, giving him a warm, inviting smile.

'Yes, indeed,' said a woman named Martha. 'We haven't had a man since... when was it, Helen?'

'1982.'

'Speak for yourselves, ladies,' a woman named Ruth chimed in. 'I had a man just last week. Or was it last year? It was quite recently, anyway.'

8

BALA COULDN'T BE SURE, BUT HE HAD THE DISTINCT FEELING Helen was flirting with him. Perhaps it was the way she smiled at him when he said, 'I've never read a book like this. Never.' Or perhaps it was the way she tapped her ringless fingers on the table and said, 'You've got such a cute accent.' He was flattered at first, but then a little disturbed. Had she seen his bald spot? Did she think he was in his fifties too? Surely he didn't look old enough to be a potential mate for her. Perhaps she was into young men. He tried to imagine being married to her. There would be pluses and minuses. She probably had a lot of experience with men. She would know that a man had certain needs and she would try to satisfy them. Whatever her mood, she would pretend to enjoy it. Rather than saying, 'I don't feel like it tonight,' she would relax, put her legs up and watch cricket with him. If she detected a slight odour, she would not complain, knowing that a man's need to watch sports is greater than his need to take a bath. She would also know that men have trouble remembering birthdays and anniversaries, that if it was up to them, the only greeting they would exchange with each other, about once a year, would be 'Happy Bathday!'

But there was a major downside to marrying her: Soon after their wedding, perhaps even *during* the wedding, his parents would definitely kill him. 'Why you are marrying a woman who is so old?' Appa would ask. 'Are you wanting a mother in America? If you had just told me, I would have sent Amma to come and live with you.' If he survived his parents' onslaught, there would be other issues to contend with. Having children would be difficult – they might need to adopt and his parents would oppose that, too. 'If you really want to adopt someone,' Amma would say, 'why not adopt your cousin Rajan? He is having trouble finding a job.'

'But Amma,' Bala would say, 'Rajan is 25. I don't want a 25-year-old son.'

'Why you are concerned about age all of a sudden? Your wife is just the right age to be Rajan's mother.'

Rajan was the older of Uncle and Aunty Ravi's two sons. He lived with his parents and spent most of the day playing the guitar and smoking beedis. He had even composed a song about beedis, the chorus of which still played occasionally in Bala's head: 'I can't do without a beedi. I'm not greedy – I'm just needy. If someone take away my beedi, I will kill them, yes, indeedy.' His apparent idleness was a source of both amusement and dismay in the family, especially since his father was an Army captain. Some relatives wondered how Captain Ravi could discipline soldiers when he couldn't even discipline his own son. His defenders, including Appa, said Ravi deserved a Medal of Honour for not using his influence to get his son an Army job. 'If he was doing that,' Appa said, 'our capital city will not be Delhi anymore – it will be Islamabad. And we will not be getting news from *The Hindu* anymore – we will be getting it from *The Muslim*.'

Bala sympathized with Ravi Uncle. He had not forced his son to get a degree in engineering, computers or some other practical field, allowing him to pursue his interests, develop his talent. As a result, Rajan had become not just a prodigy at guitar playing, but also a maestro at beedi smoking. He usually did both at the same time, prompting Bala to give him an apt nickname:

Puff Daddy. But Rajan had not heard of the rap artist and preferred to compare himself to A.R. Rahman, the popular composer whose music had enlivened countless movies. When he heard of Bala's ambition to become a film director, he made Bala promise that his first movie would feature music from a great new talent: A.R. Rajan. In the meantime, he was sending his tapes to various producers and directors, hoping to persuade one of them – perhaps even Rahman – to discover him.

Ravi Uncle had not pulled any strings to get Rajan into the Army, but far be it for him to leave his son's future to chance. When he heard that Bala was a director at an American company with an office in Chennai, he called his nephew to ask if there were any opportunities for Rajan. 'I'll try my best,' Bala said, though he knew Rajan would not be a good fit in FlexIt's customer service department, which handled calls from America. Employees were expected to speak like Americans – Rajan had enough trouble speaking like an Indian. About half the calls were from people ordering exercise machines, the other half from people complaining about them. It was important to communicate well, to make sure callers eager to buy machines shared their credit card numbers promptly, and callers eager to return them kept them anyway. Rajan would need extensive training to do the job, and even then, he'd have trouble keeping up with the other employees, most of whom were college-educated. Some were so dedicated, they had already started learning about The Flexerciser, practising responses to potential customer complaints.

Complaint: 'I've been using The Flexerciser for four weeks and seem to be gaining weight instead of losing it.'

Response: 'That could be a good sign. Just remember that muscle weighs more than fat.'

Complaint: 'I sweat a lot when I use The Flexerciser but don't feel very tired afterward.'

Response: 'I'm sorry, but did you have a complaint? It sounds like you have the body of an Olympic athlete. Have you tried running a marathon?'

Complaint: 'My husband says The Flexerciser is a piece of crap. He says I should get my money back.'

Response: 'Please tell your husband that the machine has been tested rigorously on two continents and, we are proud to say, has been found to be in compliance with all aspects of the Geneva Convention.'

The Flexerciser would hit the market in just four months. Plans for the advertising campaign were finally going smoothly. Stewart had called a senior management meeting, his face glowing like a new Ferrari.

'Good news! Good news!'

'We got McLules?' Mike asked.

'Nope, she turned us down. She's busy with her new job: sideline reporter for *Monday Night Football*. But we got someone else who's going to be great.'

'George Foreman? Don't tell me we got George Foreman!' Mike banged his fist against the table.

'No, we got someone even better: Tommy Tifatny! He's perfect.'

Tifatny was a married mechanic in his mid-forties who gained notoriety a decade ago when his teenaged girlfriend decided to introduce herself to his wife, and his wife, in turn, decided to introduce her bulldog to his girlfriend. (She survived, but barely.) The story hit the tabloids and Tifatny, intent on defending his reputation, made more appearances on *The Larry King Show*, over a period of six weeks, than Larry King himself.

'Tifatny!' Brian said. 'Why didn't I think of him?'

'Because you don't have an MBA,' John said, smiling. 'Tifatny is a great choice for several reasons. He has a well-known face, but not so well-known that we have to pay him top dollar. We don't have to Photoshop his "before" pictures, because he's already done a good job of packing it on. And his name, Tifatny, lends itself to some interesting possibilities. Just picture him in our infomercial saying, "I lost the fat, so now you can call me Tommy Tiny. Thank you very much, Flexerciser."'

'Excellent!' Stewart said. 'Tiny – I mean, Tifatny – is going to make us a lot of money. I just have a good feeling about it. Who wants to retire by the end of the year?'

Bala joined the others in raising hands and cheering. He had received a five-figure bonus last year, thanks to Le Vinsky's stellar performance, and was counting on another this year.

'Tifatny has agreed to lose 60 pounds in the next two months,' John said. 'Of course, we'll make it look like he's lost 100.'

'How's he going to lose all that extra baggage?' Brian asked.

'He's going to take a flight overseas,' Mike said. 'The airline will lose it for him.'

John laughed. 'Actually, he's undergoing surgery.'

'Is he having his stomach stapled?' Linda asked.

'No, he's having his *mouth* stapled,' John said. 'It's far more effective.'

Bala was stunned. 'How do they do that?'

'Well, it's a temporary staple and it's not too tight,' John said. 'He'll still be able to ingest liquids. And he can have the staples removed when he has lost the weight.'

Stewart shook his head. 'It's amazing what they can do today! I just heard on the news that some people are getting face transplants – instead of face lifts.'

'It's a great idea,' Mike said. 'Why lift your own face when you can lift someone else's? Soon we're going to have every kind of transplant imaginable: brain transplants, nose transplants, penis transplants.'

'That would be great,' Linda said, 'because I'm on the waiting list for a penis. It's the only way I'm going to get promoted around here.'

Stewart laughed. 'You're the only woman in the boardroom and you're complaining!' He paused for a moment, then added: 'Well, I was planning to promote you in a couple of weeks, but I might as well announce it now. Linda is no longer just Director of Human Resources. She's now also our new Plant Manager. Congratulations, Linda. Don't forget to water the ferns in the break room.'

'Thank you so much, Stewart,' Linda said. 'I can't wait to see my new paycheck.'

Bala wondered how much Linda was making. Only Stewart, Mike and the guy at the tax office knew everyone's salary. It was possible that Bala was the lowest paid manager in the room. Then again, it was also possible he was the highest. But that was unlikely, considering Brian had more experience, John had an MBA, and Mike had a Lexus. Perhaps it was good he didn't know. He was satisfied with his salary, but if he heard that Brian was making twice as much, he would suddenly be dissatisfied. It was funny how that worked – how other people's fortunes could make you feel worse about yours. It reminded him of the time, more than a decade ago, when Uncle and Aunty Balakrishnan returned from a medical conference in Singapore and gave him a Casio calculator watch. He was happy with it, wearing it proudly to school, until he heard they had bought an electronic keyboard for Rajan. 'This calculator is no good,' he complained to Appa. 'There's no sine and cosine. And it doesn't play any music.'

'*You* are no good!' Appa said angrily. 'Why you are looking gift mouth in the horse?'

Bala didn't understand why Appa was talking about horses. Had he just been reading a western? He occasionally picked up Louis L'Amour books on the street for Rs. 15. They weren't just pirated copies – they were pirated copies of pirated copies. One of them even showed the author's name as 'Louis L'Amar', perhaps to make him sound more Indian.

Appa also enjoyed watching westerns, whenever they appeared on TV. Almost any movie with a man on a horse caught his attention, especially if that man happened to be Clint Eastwood. Ravi Uncle once asked Appa what he liked so much about westerns and without hesitation Appa said, 'I like to see all the horsing around.'

Thankfully, Appa liked to watch cricket too. It was one of the few father-and-son bonding activities that Bala looked forward to (he didn't particularly care for the daily 'Let us go and pump some water' activity). Bala was impressed with Appa's knowledge of cricket – he could recall the performances of even old-timers like Hanumant Singh and Gundappa Vishwanath – and was particularly entertained with Appa's attempts at insulting players. Appa admired West Indies batsman Brian Lara, saying, 'What a first-class player!' But when Lara pounded India in a Test match, Appa yelled, 'What a first-class rascal!' Appa reserved most of his ire for the Indian team, shouting during one match: 'That

Ganguly. He is full of no talent.' Another time, when newcomer Govinder Singh allowed an English batsman to score a century, Appa shook his head and said, 'He is useless fellow. He will be the urination of the team.'

'I think you mean "ruination", Appa,' Bala said.

'Yes, urination. That is what I said.'

Bala missed watching cricket with Appa, almost as much as he missed playing cricket. No one seemed to play the game in Harrisburg. He wished he lived in a big city like New York or San Francisco, where immigrants from India, Pakistan, Guyana and other countries got together on weekends to play cricket. Perhaps he could have impressed a woman or two with his cricket skills. Alas, few American women had even heard of cricket.

'Have you ever watched cricket?' Bala asked Linda one morning.

'No,' she replied, 'but I've watched grasshoppers. Cute insects! Not as noisy as crickets. My father was an entomologist, you know.'

He pitied Americans. They thought they had it all. But without cricket, how empty their lives must be. What excitement they were missing. He wondered if it was wise to marry a woman who knew nothing about cricket, who had no appreciation for the beautiful game. She would consider it a waste of money to watch pay-per-view cricket, to spend $199 to watch the World Cup. But perhaps he would be her savior – he would rescue her from the humdrum of ordinary life and convert her into a cricket fan. She would always be grateful to him. Curling up with him on the couch, watching a cricket match, she would say, 'I can't believe I used to spend my Saturday afternoons going shopping.'

Dreaming of this possibility, he found himself itching to meet more women and decided to consult the how-to book again. It suggested he look for events organized specially for single people, such as singles dancing and singles bowling. He hadn't done much dancing in his life, but had done plenty of bowling. He was as good at bowling as he was at batting. But he knew that Americans did a different type of bowling, with an underhanded delivery and a wicket consisting of ten pins. He had seen it on TV and was willing to try it, especially since it didn't seem to involve much effort. The bowlers walked a few steps and released the ball. When the pins tumbled down, as they almost always did, the bowlers celebrated like they had climbed Mount Everest.

He scanned the *Patriot-News* for singles events and was pleased to find a listing for singles bowling, as well as one for singles tennis. But the singles tennis, to his surprise, had separate divisions for men and women. He shook his head. Tennis was out of the question. He wasn't interested in meeting single men, even if they were good at serving.

The single bowlers met every Tuesday evening at Bonnie's Billiards and Bowl, a large barn-like building in the nearby town of Dillsburg. They had reserved the five lanes on the far end, across from the video arcade. As soon as he arrived, Bala went to the vending machine and bought himself a Coke. He took tiny sips as he strode toward the group of single bowlers, 18 women and 10 men. It was an exceedingly favorable ratio. Even if all ten men found mates, there'd still be eight women left for Bala – not that he had any thoughts of moving to Utah.

A brunette named Nicole greeted him and introduced him to several others. Bala felt a little out of place. He was wearing regular white sneakers; most of the others were wearing fancy red-and-blue shoes. He hadn't realized bowling was such a formal sport. Thankfully, Nicole told him he could rent a pair of the fancy shoes for only $2. She also showed him how to put his fingers in the holes of the ball.

'Just watch what we do,' she said. 'It's easy.'

It did look easy, the way the others were rolling balls down the lanes, knocking down seven or eight pins at a time. One lanky man dropped all ten pins, shouted 'Sturiiike!' and did a cartwheel to celebrate.

'It's your turn, Bill,' Nicole said. 'Go get 'em!'

Bala took a few steps toward the lane, swung his arm backward, then brought it forward quickly in the direction of the pins, a perfect delivery except for one minor flaw: the ball was missing. It had slipped out of his grasp on the backswing and came crashing down near the seats, bouncing into one woman's ankle. She let out a little scream. A few people shrieked, others gaped at Bala. He didn't know what to do. 'I'm sorry,' he said. 'My first time.'

'It's okay,' the woman said, rubbing her ankle. 'Nothing serious.'

'I missed the target my first time, too,' the lanky man said. 'My girlfriend was not too happy!'

Everyone laughed and the tension eased, though Bala still felt a little uncomfortable. He had looked like a fool, a clumsy idiot. But he kept on bowling, reminding himself that it wasn't the most embarrassing moment of his life. There was the time in college when he accidentally knocked over his bottle of Thums Up and it spilled on his trousers, leaving a wide circle around the crotch. He had to walk around with his book bag in front of him, hoping no one would notice. He thought he had escaped detection and was beginning to relax, only to have Mr. Ganesan point at him in the middle of class and say, 'Sweating or wetting?'

Bala finished with scores of 49, 63 and 68, and was fairly satisfied with his performance, especially since the rest of his balls went forward, most of them in the correct lane. It was also a victory of sorts that by the third game, whenever he stood up, only a few people took cover. The rest had evidently gained faith in his ability.

Bala found several of the women attractive, including one who bore a striking resemblance to Rani Jeyaraj, the former Miss India. But the embarrassment of tossing the ball backwards had affected his confidence, made him more insecure than usual. And despite sipping two more Cokes, he couldn't gather the courage to make a connection with any of the women, not even Nicole, who had given four butt-slaps to another man, but none to Bala. (Perhaps the man had an exceptionally cute butt. Bala couldn't tell.)

As everyone was leaving, he approached the woman he had struck. She was quite pretty, with dirty blonde hair, aquamarine eyes and well-toned arms. She was wearing a revealing low-necked blouse and he paused for a moment to remind his eyes not to point downward.

'I'm really sorry,' he said. 'That was so clumsy of me. Hope your ankle will be okay.'

'It's fine,' she said, smiling. 'But if you really want to make it up to me, you can buy me a drink or something.'

He was dumbfounded. Was she asking him out? How could that be? Perhaps the Coke had indeed worked, made him look irresistible, covered up his clumsiness.

'Sure, why not,' he said, trying to sound nonchalant.

'Where do you want to go?'

'How about my place?'

'Your place?'

My goodness, he thought, I must have drank a lot of Coke.

She giggled. 'My Place Restaurant. It's open till midnight.'

'Oh, I see. I thought...'

'Yeah, I know,' she said, grinning. 'You thought it was going to be your lucky night.'

He felt himself blushing. 'No, not really. I just wondered how I could... you know... buy you a drink at *your* place.'

He followed her in his car, straining his foot to keep up with her speedy Celica, all the while cursing restaurant owners who tried to be too cute with names.

The restaurant was busy, packed with mostly college students. About half of them were seated in front of a huge TV screen in the dining room, watching an NBA game. Bala wanted to sit at a table, but she grabbed a stool at the bar, where a row of small TVs were all showing the same game.

'Hey Gina!' the bartender said. 'Back so soon?'

'Yeah, can't get enough of this place.'

'The usual?'

'Yeah. Who's winning?'

'The Sixers, of course. What can I get you, sir?'

'A Coke please,' Bala replied.

She contorted her face. 'Coke? Don't you drink anything other than Coke?'

'Not during the week.'

'Oh loosen up, guy. It's almost Friday.'

The bartender placed a tequila in front of her. She gulped the drink down and said, 'Another please.'

She turned to Bala: 'So whata ya do?'

'I'm a design engineer. I design exercise machines. What about you?'

'I'm a fitness trainer. I use exercise machines! Imagine that!'

His eyes widened. 'Wow! So you work at a fitness club?'

'Yeah, how did you guess? You engineers are really smart.'

'If I was smart, I would have been more careful with that bowling ball.'

'Well, those things happen. Forget about it.'

'As long as you're not going to sue me.'

'I'm not sure about that. Depends on how you behave tonight.'

She smiled and gulped another tequila down. Then, just as he was starting on his Coke, she climbed off her stool and put her lips near his ear: 'So, are you ready to go to my place now?'

9

BALA HAD NEVER BEEN WITH A WOMAN — NOT IN THAT WAY. HE had waited this long, saving himself for the special woman he would marry, and he wasn't about to give it all up for someone he had just met at a bowling alley. But it wasn't an easy decision to make. Here was an attractive woman, throwing herself at his feet, literally saying 'Take me, I'm yours,' and all he could reply was, 'It's getting late. Maybe another night,' knowing very well that there wouldn't be another night with her, not in this life, perhaps not even in the next.

When he told his friends about it, they were stunned. Mike acted like Bala had just committed a critical error in a sporting event. 'You idiot!' he said. 'You could have scored!'

Thiru didn't offer much encouragement either. 'She wanted to take *you* home?' he asked, raising his eyebrows. 'Wow, she must have been really drunk!'

Mike laughed like it was the funniest thing he had ever heard. 'I know what the problem was,' he said. '*You* were not drunk. If you had been drunk too, you would have scored. You would have hit a home run.'

'Yes,' Thiru said. 'You would have run to her home.'

Partly because of his friends' reaction, Bala had mixed feelings about his decision. But he knew he would be happy with it in the long run, especially if he found a bride soon, if he didn't have to spend many years wondering what a night with Gina would have been like. He wanted to be prepared for married life, to feel confident going to bed with his wife and doing everything he was supposed to do. But he didn't want to practise with a stranger. What was wrong, after all, with some on-the-job training? He was willing to put in overtime if necessary. He could also prepare himself in other ways, such as reading a copy of that best-selling booklet *Sex Made Easy*. From what he had heard, sex was more complicated than the biology textbooks indicated. There was something called 'foreplay', in which he was supposed to get a woman excited, perhaps by taking her on a shopping spree. Then there were various positions to choose from, including 'doggie-style' and 'missionary'. He knew what dogs did, but had never seen missionaries. Did they kneel down facing each other? Did they do it on the floor? Did they keep their clothes on? He was eager to know.

But he was getting ahead of himself. He needed to find a wife first and that was proving to be more of a challenge than he had expected. Thankfully, he had not run out of possibilities. Even Jennifer, or 'Brooke', as he still thought of her, was still in the picture. He visited Gigantic Foods several times a week, eager to go to her checkout. She smiled and greeted him like he was a good friend. But with people waiting in line, it was hard to exchange more than a few words with her. On one occasion, he said, 'Nice earrings!' and she thanked him. On another, he said, 'Nice bagging!' but she didn't seem to hear him – she was already attending to the next customer. He tried to remain optimistic. Slow progress was better than no progress. He wondered if he should send carnations again. Just as he was close to making a decision – he was leaning toward spending more money and sending roses – something happened that greatly affected their relationship: she disappeared. He went to the store morning and night, even checked the various departments – had she been promoted to the flower department or demoted to the fish department? – but could find no trace of her. Finally he asked another clerk, a friendly woman in her forties. 'Oh, she's off to college,' the clerk said. 'Shippensburg University, I believe. You're the fifth or sixth guy to ask. She was quite the popular girl.'

Bala smiled, trying to hide his disappointment. He wondered if the store was prepared for a sudden drop in sales. How could she go off to college without informing her favourite customer? But it was his fault really. He had missed an opportunity by not acting quickly. Or perhaps it was just God testing him. He remembered what Rajini had said in *Baasha*: '*Nallavangalai aandavan sothipaan; kai vida mattaan.* (Good people will be tested by God, but never discarded.)'

He wondered if he should be persistent, if he should visit Shippensburg. The university was only a 40-minute drive away. But what were the chances of running into 'Brooke' there? Perhaps he should enroll for a master's degree, an MBA or something. Then he could take evening classes and do some research in the library – re-searching for 'Brooke'.

But he wanted to get married before he turned 30, whereas 'Brooke' would probably want to wait until she graduated, as most students did. It was hard to be in two institutions at once. An institution of higher learning had tough requirements, but not as tough as the institution of marriage. At least that's what Bala had heard. Brian was always complaining about his wife's requirements, saying she was obsessed with cleanliness. He couldn't toss dirty clothes on the floor even once, couldn't leave dirty dishes in the sink even once, couldn't look at dirty magazines even once.

Perhaps 'Brooke' was too young for Bala. He had

wanted to marry a woman, not a girl, and she was just entering womanhood. Her membership card was probably still in the mail. She was ravishing, no doubt, but looks could only go so far. She might satisfy him in the bedroom, but what about all the other rooms? Would she be able to have an intelligent conversation in the living room? Would she be cultured enough to be impressed that Bala appeared to have read Rushdie?

He was having no luck with American women, no luck whatsoever, and he wondered if this was fate telling him he needed to look elsewhere. Perhaps it was his destiny to marry an Indian woman. She was out there somewhere, waiting for Bala to walk into her life. And he had better move fast, or she might settle for another man. (It was strange how destiny worked.) Inspired by this thought, he decided to be more aggressive in his quest for a bride, to search the entire world if necessary, as much of it as Google allowed him to.

As luck would have it, his Internet search for 'Indian bride' turned up dozens of matrimonial sites, with names such as Matrimonials.com, TamilMatrimony.com and HotBabesInSaris.com. Each site featured hundreds of ads, many with pictures of attractive women smiling at him. He wanted to check out as many as possible and soon found himself spending more time gazing at matrimonial ads than gazing at actual women. It was all he did at night and on weekends, sometimes even during the day at work.

There he was, absorbed in the soothing paradise of matrimonial language: 'Young, slim and attractive... highly educated... good mix of eastern and western values... enjoy cooking Indian food... great sense of humour... friends say I look like Preity Zinta.'

Then a voice suddenly shook him back to reality:

'Bala! Why are you kissing your computer?'

It was Mike, peering into Bala's office.

'Shut up, Mike! I'm not kissing it!' Bala said, pulling his face back. 'Just trying to get a closer look at this woman in a matrimonial ad. Her picture is too small.'

'Matrimonial ad? Don't tell me you're looking at matrimonial ads during work hours. Don't you know that Stewart doesn't allow us to look at anything but porn during work hours?'

Mike walked to the side of Bala's desk and leaned forward to read the ad. 'She's kinda cute,' he said. 'But definitely not as pretty as Preity. Not even close.'

'Yeah, I know. Either she's lying or her friends are. You can't believe everything you read in these ads. I heard of one woman who said she had an M.S. from Harvard, but it was just B.S.'

'So why bother with these? Getting desperate, huh?'

'Desperate? No, not me.'

'Frantic?'

'No, not frantic either.'

'Anxious?'

'No, not anxious either. Just eager.'

'Eager to get some action, huh?'

'No, eager to settle down.'

Mike shook his head. 'If you're going to settle, Bala, don't settle down – settle up! Let your mate settle down.'

Bala laughed. 'Sounds like a good idea. Got any cousins I can settle up with?'

'Only one, but she's divorced with five kids. If you're interested, let me know and I'll hook you up.'

Mike smiled and added, 'She's loaded, you know. Got two motels in the settlement. A Super 8 and a Comfort Inn. You can manage them for her. And with those five kids, you won't need employees.'

'I'll keep that in mind,' Bala said, grinning.

'Yeah, let me know and I'll make arrangements for you to get a tour of those motels. It'll be love at first sight – guaranteed!'

'Well, I'd better find *someone* soon, or my parents will insist on arranging my marriage.'

Mike shook his head. 'That's a lot of pressure, man.'

'Yeah, sort of. What about you – aren't your parents trying to arrange your marriage?'

'Arrange my marriage? Are you crazy, man? I wouldn't even let them arrange my furniture. They'd mess it all up. If you're going to be stuck with one woman for the rest of your life, you'd better know what she's like.'

'What she's like as a person?'

'No, man, what she's like in bed. What if she's a cold fish or something?'

Bala wasn't sure what Mike meant by 'cold fish'. The how-to book had also mentioned fish, saying there were 'many fish in the ocean'. But the matrimonial ads revealed little about fish. One woman said she liked to go fishing, while another said she sometimes wore fishnet stockings. But no woman called herself a 'cold fish' or 'hot fish' – or even a 'warm fish'.

10

BALA DIDN'T TELL AMMA HE WAS LOOKING AT MATRIMONIAL ads, but when he called Amma that Saturday, she encouraged him to do so. 'No harm in trying,' she said. 'What you have to lose? Sometimes you can get lucky. Look at your cousin, Rajan. He has been trying and trying and now he is going to be on the TV.'

'On TV? Really?'

'Yes, didn't I tell you? He has been chosen for new program called *Indian Idol*.'

'*Indian Idol*? Is that like *American Idol*?'

'I don't know, but no Americans will be here. Only Indians. It is *Indian Idol*.'

Bala could hear his father grumbling in the background: 'Why all these people are idle? Why they are putting idle people like Rajan on TV?'

'Idol, not idle,' Amma said.

'Idol? How Rajan can be idol? Is he going to act as Krishna or Rama?'

'No, he is going to be singing and playing his guitar.'

'He must be really excited,' Bala said.

'We all are excited. He is trying and trying and finally he is succeeding.'

'Maybe I should have kept trying too – trying to be a film director.'

'No, no, kanna, that is not what I am saying. It is okay for Rajan – he is not so intelligent like you. All I am saying is, sometimes it is good to keep trying. You must try to look at matrimonial ads. If you are not finding good girls, then you must come to India. I will find you some nice, sweet ones that...'

'Yes, Amma, I know.'

It was like a threat, one that made Bala look at matrimonial ads with more urgency than before. He bookmarked 25 matrimonial sites, including IndianUnions.com, not realizing until later that it focused on the type of unions that employers disliked. He found the ads engrossing, even addictive, though they were often puzzling too, leaving him with several unanswered questions:

(1) What did people mean when they said they'd had an *innocent* divorce? No one ever said they'd had a *guilty* divorce. Perhaps that was because people considered marriage a life sentence. You had to be innocent to be released. Or perhaps the divorce court judge had made a ruling like this: 'After considering all the evidence, I find you, Mohan, completely innocent. You have been unjustly punished. Guards, please set him free from this marriage. But I find you, Sharmila, guilty as charged. You deserve to be punished. I sentence you to three more marriages. Guards, introduce her immediately to the man from the previous case.'

(2) If someone was a single doctor, was there some kind of law that required them to marry another doctor? Bala had come across so many ads in which doctors said they were seeking other doctors. That confused him. Did they want to get married or were they trying to open a clinic? Doctors marrying doctors seemed so unfair, because it deprived everyone else of free medical attention. Some doctors, perhaps desperate to get married, were willing to consider engineers, computer programmers and other professionals who fell into the category of 'not doctors but still making good money'. But many still insisted on

marrying within their profession. Just once in his life, Bala wanted to see an ad that said: *Parents of a 26-year-old physician girl, educated at top medical college, beautiful, fair, Hindu, u.s. citizen, seeking responses from qualified janitors, truckers and waiters. Preference will be given to those with only a high-school diploma.*

(3) Why did people list the qualifications of their relatives? *My brother is a medical doctor, my father is an engineer, my sister is a software professional, my uncle is an accountant, my aunt is a professor, I myself am a high-school dropout.*

Despite such baffling questions, Bala was determined to read as many ads as possible. He even printed some of them to read in the bathroom. That was easier than carrying his laptop there. A few of the ads were quite creative. One woman seemed to be a fan of Shakespeare: *What man art thou that, owning a computer, thou hast not sent me an email? Dost thou not want to meet this slim attractive lady with a Ph.D. in Renaissance Studies? If thou playeth with my affections, I'll frown, and be hurt, and send my papa to kick thine butt.*

One seemed to be neither this nor that: *I'm neither tall nor short, neither fat nor skinny, neither fair nor dark. I'm neither rich nor poor, neither beautiful nor ugly, neither outgoing nor reserved. If you're neither a doctor nor an engineer, please email me neither today nor tomorrow.*

One seemed to be fairly enlightened: *I possess the best of Indian values with a great amount of modern thinking mixed in. I believe in taking care of parents and the elderly. I believe in equality of the sexes, both at home and at work. I do not believe in dowry. If you agree with these values, you might be the right man* for me, as long as you are a Tamil Iyengar, preferably Vadakalai too. Write to me and we can see if our horoscopes match.

One seemed to be fairly lightened: *My looks are quite different from most South Indians. I'm not dark at all. My complexion is white – whiter than many white people. My friends even call me Snow White. It is sometimes a burden, being so fair, because strangers are always stopping me to ask what cream I use. But I have not tried any cream in my entire life, except of course ice cream.*

One seemed to be multi-talented: *I am a doctor, musician and writer. As a doctor, I specialize in homeopathic medicine. It is the best, most effective way to heal people. When I am not practising medicine, I am usually practising the sitar. I've played it at various public events, receiving many standing ovations. I am a writer too – I have written numerous comments on Internet blogs. I've received many compliments on my comments and hope to publish a collection of them one day.*

About a third of the ads had been placed by parents. Some seemed quite eager to get their daughters married: *Parents of a 28-year-old Tamil girl, well-educated, fair, beautiful, must-see-to-appreciate, seeking responses from engineers, doctors and employed computer programmers. Serious inquiries only, all arrangements final, no returns or exchanges.*

Some seemed to know exactly what they needed in a groom: *The boy must be fair (very fair a plus!) and intelligent. He must be handsome or at least earning a handsome salary. He must be between the ages of 26 and 29, at least 5'8', and no more than 180 pounds. He must have a good heart, with a pulse of 60 or lower.*

His blood pressure must be no higher than 120/80. He must have a full set of teeth, all his hair and no missing fingers or toes. He must be a non-drinker, non-smoker and non-vegetarian. He must be a good Christian with good values and a good car.

Some seemed to have daughters who were simply superlative: *Our daughter is very fair, very slim and very homely. She is educated at very good university and has very good job. She is also very healthy, with no illnesses or diseases, as far as we know.*

Now and then, out of sheer curiosity, Bala also browsed the ads of eligible men. He wanted to evaluate the competition, see what other men had to offer. He was always careful to close the door of his office. He didn't want someone to walk in and think he was gay. It was okay to be gay, as long as you were comfortable with it, like John and many others. But Bala was only comfortable being straight. He even felt uneasy when Thiru touched him: patted his back, rubbed his shoulders or gave him one of those bear hugs that only bears ought to be giving. It wasn't that Bala didn't appreciate his friend's affection; it was just that he wondered what other people might think. Thiru, in contrast, seemed oblivious. If he felt like putting his arm around Bala, he would go ahead and do it, even if they happened to be sitting in the front row of the *Oprah Winfrey Show*. Thiru would probably raise his hand and try to answer one of Oprah's questions, while his other hand remained squarely on Bala's shoulder. He might even pull Bala closer, as if to tell the world, 'This is my best friend, I love him and I don't care what you morons think.' Bala, meanwhile, would suffer a neck injury, trying to turn his head away from the camera.

At times, Bala wished he could be like Thiru. There

was nothing wrong with men showing affection to each other. It was probably a healthy thing, as good for a man as eating carrots or doing sit-ups. But in America, heterosexual men rarely touched each other, except during sporting events, when it was perfectly acceptable for them to embrace, slap butts, or bump chests. As long as they were playing sports, no one questioned their sexuality, no one wondered if the basketball court was the only place they made passes to each other. Women, on the other hand, were free to show as much affection as they wanted to each other: hold hands, hug, even French kiss. At one night club, Bala watched in amazement as two women went out on the dance floor, bumped their bodies against each other for a good twenty minutes, then returned to their table and kissed their husbands.

Bala couldn't imagine dancing like that with Thiru, not even if his friend shaved his moustache. Perhaps Bala just wasn't secure enough in his masculinity. He certainly didn't feel as confident as some of the men whose matrimonial ads he was browsing. He found a few ads rather intimidating. One man seemed to have better looks and a better salary: *I am a model accountant. When I'm not working on numbers, I'm posing for pictures. With my good looks, I've done quite a lot of modeling. I am also a certified public accountant (cpa), certified financial planner (cfp) and certified loophole finder (clf). I earn $90,000 p.a., not including what I get from appearing in the annual 'Hot Accountants' calendar. I enjoy looking at figures – and not just those of my female clients. Despite my many achievements and accomplishments, too many to mention here, I am very modest and humble. In fact, if there was an award for modest men, I would get it.*

One man seemed to be more intelligent: *I have an IQ of 160, which is higher than 99.999% of the general population. I am able to solve mathematical problems very quickly. I am also able to memorize a great deal of information. Not to brag, but I have memorized the names of all the men who were once married to Elizabeth Taylor.*

One man seemed to be better house-trained: *I am very different from most men. I like to cook and clean. My cooking skills are as good as my mother's. That's because she trained me. You name it, I can make it: idli, dosa, sambhar, payasam, puris, etc. I bet your mouth is already watering. (It might be wise to step back from your keyboard.) My mother also trained me to keep things clean. My apartment is so clean that you can eat off the kitchen floor. (Just ask my dog.) All my friends say that the woman who marries me will be very lucky. She will get herself a very good houseband.*

Bala wondered if he could compete with these men. But he told himself that there was one woman out there for him, one woman who would find him as irresistible as lemonade on a hot day. He didn't have to impress the entire female species – he just had to make one woman think he was special. Perhaps this woman had placed an ad and was waiting for him to respond. Waiting months or even years. Checking her email daily and silently cursing Bala for not finding her ad.

He tried to look for ads that seemed to be written for him, but didn't have much luck – until one fine morning when he stumbled upon a rather obscure website: ImFreakingAlmost30.com. A featured ad on the site made him jump out of his seat:

I'm 28 years old and will soon graduate with an MBA from Kellogg (the business school, not the cereal company). My hobbies include dancing (bharatnatyam mostly, though I occasionally hit the clubs), cooking (mostly South Indian cuisine, though I've dabbled in Chinese) and watching cricket (every chance I get). I'm quite crazy about cricket, like most women are crazy about shopping. (In fact, when my uncle told me he wanted to fix a match for me, I thought he was talking about cricket.) My father is a big cricket fan and, though I grew up (and still live) in Chicago, I became addicted to the game too. I even play it recreationally with my brother and his friends. My brother says I'm the best cricket player in America who also dances bharatnatyam.

I'm searching for a tall, professional man, working in the U.S. or Canada, who is close to his family and will make his wife and children his main priority in life, aside from cricket. (As you can guess, my family is important to me.) Your looks do matter to me (we must have some chemistry, before we can proceed to physics and biology). However, speaking as a fun-loving woman, let me say that a man with a great personality and sense of humour is hard to resist. Why not give it a shot and see what destiny has in store for us? Just send me an email, along with your picture, and we'll take it from there.

She had scored well in the three C's Bala was hoping for: character, cooking and cricket. And as a bonus, she didn't seem concerned about the other C's: caste, complexion and chicken-eating. He never expected to find a woman who was crazy about cricket, but now that he had, he considered it a major plus, icing on the cake, almonds in the payasam. She was also quite pretty, though the picture she had posted was a little grainy. It seemed to have been cut from a group picture. Either that or there was an arm growing out of her head. Bala had seen many of these cropped pictures – one woman even appeared to be wearing a wedding dress – and couldn't help wondering how long it had taken these women to find a picture they looked good in. But this picture didn't really bother him. If necessary, they could have the arm surgically removed.

He wondered if he should send her a picture of similar quality or a high-resolution portrait. He browsed all the pictures in his laptop and quickly eliminated several of them – the close-up shots of the moon. He didn't want to give her an astronomical scare. It was important to show his best side first, then introduce the less appealing side gradually, after their relationship was on solid footing.

After much deliberation, he settled on a picture that was several years old, but seemed like the type of shot that would impress her. Not only was he holding a cricket bat, he looked trim and fit, about 30 pounds lighter. He wondered for a moment if he was deceiving her, but brushed the thought aside. He hadn't retouched the picture after all. With his Photoshop skills, he could have made himself even lighter. He could have lost all the pigment in his skin. He could have made himself as fair as a polar bear. But he would have felt uneasy about that. He preferred to be himself – a grizzly bear. It didn't matter that people considered him 'dark' and 'dusky', that in the group picture of his engineering batch, he was the set of teeth in the back. He was comfortable with his complexion and had no desire to change it. If dark skin was good enough for Rajini, it was good enough for him. What he did want to change, however, was his weight. Could he lose 30 pounds before he met her? It was certainly possible, especially if he went on a fast.

He could limit himself to just fast food. A McChicken sandwich for lunch, a burrito for dinner and soon he'd be a lot thinner. If he lost the weight before he met her, she wouldn't care that the picture was old. It would be a good way to motivate himself: lose the weight or lose the woman. As meticulous as he was in choosing the picture, he was even more careful in composing the email. It was important to get the words right.

Hi! My name is Bala. I saw your ad and liked what you wrote. I am a big cricket fan too. I've also tried to cook a little, but if you asked me to name my favourite dish, I would have to say 'satellite dish'. That's how I watch cricket. I like to watch Tamil movies too, especially the ones with superstar Rajinikanth. I grew up in Chennai, came to America five years back and am working in Harrisburg, Pennsylvania, as Director of Design Engineering at a company that makes exercise machines. I have a black Labrador retriever who is good at fetching things from all over my neighbourhood (I don't have to subscribe to the newspaper). You say you're looking for a tall man. Well, I'm 5'7', tall enough to change a light bulb for you – as long as you have a step ladder. By the way, my younger sister, Chitra, likes bharatnatyam too. Maybe you can give her some lessons! Looking forward to your reply.

The next day, Bala checked his Yahoo email account 163 times – and that was before lunch. He would have checked it more, but Stewart insisted he attend a meeting. On the 164th try, just after he returned from the board room, he received a reply from her:

Hi there! Thank you for your email. You sound like a great guy, but unfortunately I'm looking for someone who was born in America or at least grew up here. Good luck in your search! Kaavya.

11

BALA RETURNED TO THE MATRIMONIAL WEBSITE AND READ her ad again just to make sure he hadn't missed any lines. Perhaps he overlooked the line that said, 'Please note that I'd prefer to marry a man who grew up in America and can put up with a big snob like me.' Had she really rejected him because he grew up in India, this woman who played cricket and danced bharatnatyam? What did she think – that he didn't wash his balls? (He always did. It was something his cricket coach in high school had preached: 'Boys, always keep your balls and bats clean.') Perhaps she was looking for a man who spoke with an American accent, wore shorts to the grocery store, and ate dosas with a fork and knife.

It was early afternoon and he didn't feel like working anymore. His mind was so full of resentment and disappointment that the positive feelings from the meeting had all but dissipated. John had announced that the taping of the infomercial in New York had gone well, so well that if the Academy of Motion Pictures awarded Oscars for infomercials, Tifatny would be a shoo-in for 'Best Actor in a Misleading Role'. Not only had he performed well, he had been genuinely impressed with The Flexerciser and asked if he could take it home. John had promised to ship another one to him. It was customary for FlexIt Inc. to keep the model used in the infomercial, so it could be auctioned off on eBay to benefit a local charity, such as FDF (FlexIt Doughnut Fund). Annika Le Vinsky's Flex-appeal machine, which retailed for $199, fetched a high bid of $13,500, allowing the company to not only replenish the doughnut fund, but also provide a feast for the homeless in Harrisburg during Thanksgiving and Christmas, making Bala wonder how homeless people survived the rest of the year – did they go into hibernation?

He tried to recall what else had transpired at the meeting, but his thoughts kept returning to the Chicago woman. Who did she think she was, rejecting him because he had grown up in India? Did she think she was somehow superior to him? Didn't she know that India gives a person unique experiences and perspectives, that you haven't really lived until you've experienced rush-hour traffic in Chennai? Poor woman – she had missed out on so much. She didn't know the pleasure of drinking sugarcane juice on a sweltering day, of playing gili-danda in the street, of getting your eardrums shattered during Deepavali. She had never taken a bath outdoors, never soaped herself during a monsoon rain. She had never sat in a packed theatre to watch a Rajinikanth movie, never heard the wild cheers when he thrashes a villain with such amazing skill that even Gandhi would have applauded.

Indians like her were all too common in America, the type who thumbed their noses at anyone fresh from the motherland. Bala had heard the term 'ABCD' and he finally realized what it stood for: American-born condescending dumbass. But not all Indian-Americans were ABCDS. Many were EFGHS (easygoing, fair-minded, generous humans). If only there was an easy way to tell them apart, an easy way to protect himself from being summarily rejected again. Perhaps he needed to post an ad himself and emphasize his Indian upbringing. That way, only broad-minded women would respond, the ones who had either grown up in India themselves or were willing to focus on more important issues, such as whether their future husbands knew how to change a tyre.

Bala went to the 'Create an ad' section of the website and read the instructions. First, he needed to agree to a long list of terms and conditions, protecting the website from every possible outcome. He could not, for example, sue the website if he discovered on his wedding night that his new wife, the one he had met through a matrimonial ad, was actually a man. Nor could he sue the website if she turned out to be a lesbian, a transvestite, or an Amway rep.

After agreeing to the conditions, he entered his Citibank Visa number and paid $20 for the ad. He was promptly taken to another page, where he had to fill out several blank spaces, providing vital details about himself, including age (29), height (medium), profession (engineer), religion (Hindu) and sex (not yet). Then he confronted a large rectangular box. What could he say about himself? He leaned forward in his swivel chair, shoulders slouched, and pecked at the keyboard with his index fingers, pausing after each sentence to evaluate it.

I'm a true gentleman, like Sidney Poitier and Cary Grant combined. No, that made him sound old.

I'm a well-settled, well-educated professional who has a good blend of eastern and western values. No, that sounded too much like other ads he had read. Besides, his values were more eastern than western, especially considering how much he valued Rajini movies.

I'm tall, dark and handsome, own a dot-com company and have enough money to hire Mukesh Ambani as my butler. He chuckled. If only. The women would be lined up all the way to Delhi.

I'm a smart, well-educated engineer who has a great sense of humour. That was much better, if stretching the truth a little. Bala did have a pretty good sense of humour. That's why he enjoyed walking through Sanjay's Rice and Spice Shop. The owner, Sanjay Taneja, had written all the signs in the produce section himself, signs such as 'cook cumber', 'calling flower' and 'what a melon'. Near the exit was another sign: 'Please come and gain.'

I grew up and received all my education in India, so I'm very much an Indian at heart, though I've taken quite a liking to America. I really enjoy taking him for walks. (He's my Labrador retriever and I named him America in honour of my new country.) He hoped to meet a woman who liked dogs. If she preferred cats, their relationship would be doomed from the start. He'd be better off marrying someone from another planet.

I enjoy sports, particularly cricket, Tamil movies (Rajinikanth is my favourite) and Scrabble. I am an avid reader and am currently working on Midnight's Children *by Salman Rushdie.* He had certainly started working on the novel, occasionally putting his laptop on it. He hadn't played Scrabble in years, but it was important to show his intellectual side. Playing Scrabble was just a notch or two below playing chess, which was a notch or two below reading Rushdie. Uncle and Aunty Balakrishnan had bought him a Scrabble set when he was only 10 and he was soon beating everyone in the family, partly because he was always so lucky: no one else wanted to keep score.

I consider myself a family man and will treat my wife like a princess. She will be a special part of my life. Such sentiments seemed trite, but Bala couldn't avoid them. He wanted his future wife to know he

would treat her well. He would take her for dinner, take
her for movies, but never take her for granted.

*I'm looking for a woman who's smart, attractive,
loving and considerate. Language, caste and
complexion are not concerns for me, but you must
have a sense of humour.* If his bride were dark-skinned,
it wouldn't bother him, but he knew his mother and
relatives would grumble and gossip, as though any of
them were visible at night.

He read the ad five times and, holding his breath, hit
the 'submit' button. A message in block letters appeared:
'Thank you for using ImFreakingAlmost30.com. Your
ad will appear online within 24 hours, as soon as it has
been reviewed by our staff. We wish you luck in finding
the perfect mate. Please let us know the outcome of your
matrimonial search. If you're successful, we'll feature
you on our Success Stories page. And if you aren't, we'll
give you a free ad for one full year on our other website:
ImFreakingAlmost40.com.'

At least fifty times a day, Bala checked his Yahoo
mailbox, hoping to receive more than just the usual
string of junk email. But almost every time, when he
scrolled through his inbox, he let out a groan. There
were the requisite letters from people in Nigeria and
other parts of the world who needed his help and
were eager to transfer millions of dollars into his bank
account (Bala wished he could transfer millions of brain
cells into their heads). There were the jokes and funny
pictures forwarded from one friend to another, until
they had crisscrossed the planet thousands of times.
And there were the numerous emails offering miracle
products, including one whose subject line – 'Add three
inches' – grabbed Bala's attention, but whose contents
disappointed him. He wanted to be taller, not longer.

After three weeks, he had gathered a smattering of email from hopeful women or their families, but none that excited him. A New York woman seemed to be having trouble with English. *Myself Sarita, looking for man to husband. I good woman, nice and cooking well. You like, you reply please. I be waiting near computer.*

A Florida man seeking a groom for his younger sister in India provided a list of his family's accomplishments. *My father who passed away three years ago worked in Chennai for United Nations. My older sister is a software engineer for CTC in Chennai. Her husband is a highly qualified surgeon, world-renowned throughout India.*

A Pondicherry woman sent him only her 'bio-data'. *DOB: June 14, 1979. Degrees: B.A. in Literature, M.A. in Marketing. Languages: Tamil, Hindi, English and a little French. Hobbies: Cooking, sewing and playing carom. References: Available upon request.*

He was beginning to think the ad was a complete waste, no better than scribbling his phone number on the backside of a cow. Perhaps all the good women were taken, leaving leftovers for men like him. Or perhaps they were too sophisticated, too classy to browse the Internet for mates. He soon found himself checking his email with less anticipation, sometimes going a whole half-hour without scanning his inbox.

Then one day it arrived, an email that made him feel like climbing on his desk and dancing. He read it three times, savouring the words, congratulating himself on his good fortune.

Hi Rajinikanth fan! You sound so much like me, it's amazing. I'm a 27-year-old attorney in Washington, D.C. I'm 5-foot-3, slim and medium-complexioned.

*People have told me I'm very pretty, but you'll have to
be the judge of that... Like you, I enjoy Tamil movies,
though my favourite actor is Kamal Haasan. (He
doesn't have five 'A's in his name for nothing.)... I have
a dog too, a sheepdog named Serenity (she's very
friendly). Hope to hear from you. Uma.*

Bala was eager to chat with her, but had to first send
an email requesting her number. The next evening,
just before dinner, he turned on his laptop and was
delighted to see a reply from Uma in the midst of some
junk email. Along with her number, she had written:
*Call me any evening. Looking forward to talking to
you. Hugs, Uma.*

He liked 'hugs', liked how this light, compact word
could carry so much warmth. As he dialled her number,
he tried to imagine her hugging him. It would be nicer
than one of those hugs Thiru gave him – longer, warmer
and better smelling.

She answered the phone on the first ring and he felt
a tingle in his neck. Her voice was sweet, almost lyrical,
yet as confident as an attorney's.

'Hi Bala, I'm so glad you called.' He wanted to pause
and absorb the words, feel their texture, inhale their
scent.

They spoke for hours, as excitedly as friends at a
reunion. The conversation was so smooth, so effortless
that Bala wondered if they had spoken before, if they
had known each other as children. He was astounded to
learn that when Uma was 12, her family had spent a year
in Anna Nagar, just two streets away from his house. He
and Uma had probably drunk water delivered by the
same truck. They had an H_2O connection. If that wasn't
amazing enough, they discovered another surprising
link: Bala's engineering professor, Mr. Ganesan, was

Uma's mother's second cousin's husband's nephew's wife's uncle. Or something like that. It was too confusing for Bala to follow, but he exclaimed, 'What a small world! You're related to my favourite professor!'

'Related by marriage. I've met him only once, when I was thinking of doing engineering. He said he could help me get admission.'

'Yes, he is a very helpful man. Helpful and brilliant. My friends and I were always discussing his brilliance.'

Bala was glad Uma was related to Mr. Ganesan only by marriage. Otherwise their children, if they got married, might inherit a double dose of baldness genes.

They chatted until midnight – Bala forgot all about eating dinner – and arranged to speak again the following evening. Halfway through their second chat, Uma invited Bala to visit her, surprising him with her forwardness. 'So soon?' he asked, trying to appear calm, searching for a reason to delay their meeting. He didn't want to rush things. If she had started to like him by phone, wouldn't time only deepen her feelings? If they spoke a few more times, perhaps she would fall madly and irreversibly in love with him. He had heard of people who fell in love on the Internet, even without hearing each other's voice. But it would be wiser, he knew, to find out what Uma was like in person, before getting too attached to her. What if she didn't really own a dog? What if she was actually 5-foot-9? What if she had a picture of Himesh Reshammiya on her wall?

They decided to meet the following Saturday for lunch. Uma asked Bala if he'd like to bring America along. 'That's a great idea,' he said. 'I'm sure America would really like to get to know Serenity.' If the two dogs hit it off, that would be a good sign for their owners. Perhaps they could have a double wedding. America did seem to need some female companionship. Not only had he been getting a little too amorous with Bala's leg, he had been having a torrid affair with Bala's pillow. Bala would come home to find America having his way with the pillow on the bedroom floor. 'Relax, you idiot, it's only a pillow,' Bala said one day, but then he saw the look in America's eyes and realized what the dog was probably thinking: 'Easy for you to say, buddy. You get to sleep with it every night.'

When Bala told Mike about his upcoming date with Uma, Mike acted like Bala had just picked someone up in cyberspace. 'Is she a hottie? One of those Internet babes?'

Bala smiled. 'As pretty as Preity, I'm sure.'

'Good luck, man! Make sure you take some protection with you.'

'Protection? I'm taking America with me.'

Mike burst out laughing. 'No, man. I mean condoms. You never know, you might get lucky.'

'You're crazy, Mike,' Bala said, shaking his head. He hoped to get lucky, but not in the way Mike was thinking. He wanted to be lucky for the rest of his life, not just for ten minutes. 'We're having lunch, that's all.'

'Well, it might be a three-course meal. An appetizer for the first course, then the main course, and then intercourse.'

'You really are crazy, Mike,' Bala said, laughing. 'Intercourse is out of the question. I'll be lucky if I get outercourse.'

He didn't tell anyone else at work about Uma, but he didn't need to. Mike was a one-man broadcasting network. Within a few hours everyone was asking about Bala's 'hot Internet date'.

'You met her on the Net?' John asked. 'Isn't that risky?'

'No, John, I met her through a matrimonial ad. Everyone does it. I mean, lots of Indians do it. We've been using matrimonial ads for ages.' He explained how the first matrimonial ads appeared millions of years ago in caves in India. Cavemen etched pictures of the type of cavewoman they wanted to marry, usually one with wide hips who could survive childbirth. Some cavemen drew large breasts, but most wanted their wives to be as upright as possible.

'Nowadays, you can find matrimonials in every Indian newspaper and on many websites,' Bala said.

'Do they have matrimonials for gay people?'

'No, I don't think so, John. You've got to give them time. This is only the 21st century, you know.'

Bala didn't have the heart to tell John that homosexuality was outlawed in India. There was no need to. John would not be travelling to India anytime soon. Bala didn't want his friend to have a negative impression of India, not when there was a technological explosion going on and everyone was speaking so positively about his motherland. He had just seen a *Time* magazine with Salman Rushdie's ex-wife, the model and actress Padma Lakshmi, on the cover, along with the title: 'India blossoms'. India was apparently blossoming with not just technology, but also beautiful women.

12

BALA AWOKE AT 8 A.M. ON SATURDAY, AN HOUR EARLIER than usual. He needed to get ready for the date. He scoured his closet and selected a pair of navy blue Dockers and a striped knit shirt. He showered and shaved, trimmed his moustache, and applied a few drops of Old Spice to his chin and a little more to his chest. Slipping into his outfit, he admired himself in the full-length mirror. He parted his lips in a restrained smile and held the expression for half a minute, practising the look he would present Uma. He wanted to look happy to see her, but not so happy she might think he was a nutcase.

He tried to get America to sit in the front of the car, but the dog jumped to the backseat. He seemed to like it there, perhaps because he could stick his head out of the window and look like an important dog, being driven around by a chauffeur. Indeed, when they passed the neighbourhood beagle going for a walk with its owner, America barked louder than usual, as if to say, 'Tally ho old chap! I'm off to get some wine and cheese.' Bala hoped America would behave himself at Uma's, would try to control his appetite and male urges.

It took them a little over two hours to drive to the D.C. suburb of Rockville, Maryland, where Uma owned a townhouse. Pulling into her development, Bala glanced in the mirror and skimmed his hand over his hair, making sure the breeze hadn't exposed too much of his scalp. The townhouses looked elegant and new, with screened porches and large bay windows. Midway down a cul-de-sac, he found Uma's home, a cluster of azaleas flanking the driveway. The lawn seemed a little overgrown and as Bala walked to the door, America by his side, he imagined himself mowing it for her, every Saturday for the rest of their lives. She would admire him through the bay window, his muscles tensing and relaxing, snips of grass clinging to his bare chest. There would be no sign of the extra weight he once carried. In fact, the neighbours would be shocked to learn that he had never once competed in the Olympics.

Before he could ring the doorbell, she appeared before him, all frizzy-haired and glowing, his practised smile wilting in surprise. He held out a spray of pink carnations, but she swept past them, intent on giving him a hug. Her forehead brushed against his cheek and he felt a strong impulse to kiss it, but before he could act, she pulled away and turned her attention to America. 'What a beautiful dog,' she said, bending down to pet him, giving him so much affection, Bala felt the urge to get on his hands and knees and bark.

America wagged his tail and then, as though trying to show Bala how it was done, started licking Uma's cheek. She giggled and said, 'You like me! What a cute dog you are!' As she rose and turned to the door, a series of high-pitched barks came from inside the house, followed by a long growl from America. Uma opened the door and the sheepdog came bursting out, heading straight for Bala's legs. He froze and experienced a momentary flashback: the dog in Chennai lunging at him. The sheepdog jumped and put her paws on Bala's thighs, swishing her tail vigorously. He was relieved to see that she meant no harm, but was merely welcoming him to the house. 'Down, Serenity, down!' Uma yelled. The dog slid down, took a step toward America, then changed her mind and scampered to Uma. America had stopped growling, his face projecting a look of utter curiosity. He followed Serenity into the house and proceeded to do what Bala had feared: inspect the sheepdog's rear end. Bala was embarrassed. Would Uma think poorly of him that he hadn't trained his dog to control his urges? To make matters worse, Serenity was staring at Uma, seemingly oblivious to the nose pressed into her behind. It wasn't a good sign: America was interested in Serenity, but Serenity seemed to be indifferent to America.

Thankfully, Uma was busy searching for a vase to put the carnations in and hadn't noticed America's moves. She looked even better than Bala had imagined – high cheekbones, shapely chin, mermaid hips squeezed into faded jeans. She was one of those women who seemed to put no effort into their appearance, who seemed to be attractive totally by accident. Even if you pulled them out of a burning building, they would look enchanting with their charred hair and scorched eyebrows.

Uma showed Bala around her home, each room a tasteful blend of contemporary furniture and art, all light wood and pastel prints. Bala felt like he was getting a private tour through IKEA. Leafy philodendrons, set in patterned terra cotta, enlivened the decor. A candle in the bathroom sent wafts of cherry down the hallway. It made Bala think about his home and the type of smell that would waft down the hallway from the bathroom.

'Your place is so much nicer than mine,' he said.

'Really?' she intoned and he wondered if he had said the wrong thing.

A studio portrait of her family – parents and three children – adorned the living room wall, beside a framed outline of the Mahatma at a spinning wheel. (No picture of Himesh Reshammiya, thankfully.) Uma's triple-deck stereo caught Bala's eye and he hunched over to browse her CD collection. Marley, Lennon, Shankar, Yankovic – all the giants of music were there.

'My cousin is a musician,' Bala said. 'He's even singing on *Indian Idol*. My mother just told me he has reached the top ten. Everyone in Tamil Nadu is voting for him.'

'You mean A.R. Rajan?'

'You've heard of him? Oh my God!'

'Of course, I've heard of him. He's all over the Net. Haven't you seen all those fan websites? He's even on that popular site HotTamilGuys.com. I can't believe he's your cousin!'

Bala couldn't believe he had missed all those websites. He had been so busy looking at matrimonial ads, he hadn't bothered to google Rajan. Was he really such a big star? Even Uma seemed to be enthralled by him. Bala spent a few minutes telling her all about Rajan, how he hadn't gone to college but had instead put all his energy into guitar-playing and beedi-smoking.

'Nobody thought he would be a success in life,' Bala said.

'Not even you?'

'Well, I thought that, with a lot of practice, he might one day be able to work at a call centre.'

Uma smiled. 'I'm sure his phone is ringing off the hook now.'

She sat across from him at the dining table. She had prepared some of his favourites: chapatis, chicken curry, aloo and fried eggplant. 'The eggplant is absolutely delicious,' he said. 'As good as my mother's.'

She chuckled. 'Oh, it'll never be as good as mommy's.'

As he was reaching for a second helping of eggplant,

his elbow bumped his glass of water. It was only half-full, but seemed to splash across a third of the tablecloth – and part of Uma's shirt. 'I'm so sorry,' he said. 'Very clumsy of me.'

'That's okay,' she said. 'It's only water.'

They moved to the living room for dessert, vermicelli payasam, another of his favourites. Bala sat on a beige divan and was glad to see Uma coming to sit beside him, rather than taking the leather armchair across the room. Perhaps he could put his arm around her. But as soon as she sat down, a bundle of fur bounded over and filled the space between them. The sheepdog angled her body toward Bala and lowered her head onto his thigh, expecting to be petted. 'I think she likes you,' Uma said. Bala was hardly thrilled. This wasn't the female he had been hoping to pet. Everything seemed to be mixed up: Serenity liked Bala, who liked Uma, who liked America, who liked Serenity.

Uma turned, lifted her legs onto the divan and leaned back against the armrest. She rubbed Serenity's underside with her toes. The wet splotch on her shirt made the underside of her bra visible and aroused Bala. He tried to distract himself.

'You've got pretty feet,' he said, looking over the furry barrier at them. Uma smiled, then steered the conversation in another direction. She hadn't been to India in 11 years, what about him?

'It's been five years for me. I want to visit soon, because my grandfather is almost 90. If I don't go and see him soon, he says he won't talk to me for the next 20 years.'

'I'd like to go back too. I hear things have changed a lot.'

'You'll be amazed. My mother says that everyone

has a cell phone these days, even some of the beggars on the street. That's how they keep in touch with their investment brokers.'

Uma laughed. 'Some of our family friends are returning to India. They've been here for ten years, got their green cards, and have decided to go back. They say they can live better there.'

'It doesn't surprise me. You should see how my uncle and aunty in Thoothukudi live. They have a bigger staff than the Ritz-Carlton. They have cars, but don't do the driving. They have clothes, but don't do the washing. They have noses, but don't do the picking.'

Uma smiled. 'I don't know if I could live like that. I don't know if I could have even just one servant.'

'Oh, you'd get used to it. I mean, don't you ever wish you didn't have to do the dishes?'

'Yeah, I do. That's why I have an automatic dishwasher.'

'My aunt has one too. She just snaps her fingers and he automatically does the dishes.'

They chatted for half an hour, then spent the rest of the afternoon watching a movie Uma had rented: *Hey Ram*, starring Kamal Haasan and Shahrukh Khan.

'Shahrukh is nothing compared to Kamal Haasan,' Uma said. 'He can't even grow a good moustache. Even yours is better.'

'Hundred times better!' Bala said. He didn't like the way Uma had said 'even yours', as though he was a teenage boy who had just sprouted a few hairs. But it was his fault, really. He had made a mistake that morning, trimming his moustache. If he had known Uma was into moustaches, he could have grown a long bristly one to sweep her off her feet.

'I grew my first moustache when I was 10,' he said,

hoping to impress her.

'Really? My brother had a moustache when he was 9.'

'Well, I have to trim mine every day.'

'My brother does it twice a day. And he uses garden shears.'

Bala laughed and shook his head. He didn't know what to say. Uma's brother was apparently blessed with superior moustache genes.

When the movie ended, he got up and said, 'I guess I should get going.' He wanted to stay longer, but Uma hadn't invited him for supper. All she said was, 'Yeah, you have a very long drive,' as though he was heading to Florida.

As they said goodbye outside, he felt like kissing her, but couldn't gather the nerve. 'It was so nice meeting you,' she said, putting her arms around America. Bala tried to do the same, but Serenity had evidently grown tired of him and was sitting by the door. Almost the entire afternoon, she had sat on the couch beside Bala, ignoring poor America, who had to sit alone on the floor and wonder why Uma wasn't moving over to make room for him.

The next day, Bala couldn't stop thinking of Uma. Did she like him as much as he liked her? Would they soon be planning a wedding? How long would he need to grow his moustache?

Eager to speak to her, he called that evening, raving again about her cooking, how much he missed it already. She thanked him and asked about his drive home, did he run into much traffic? Just hearing her voice, her concern, filled him with pleasure.

'I have something to tell you,' she said after a minute, and his heart jumped. Would she reveal her feelings for him?

'I don't know if this is going to work out. I didn't really feel any sparks yesterday. What about you?'

'Uh... no, not really.'

Sparks? What were these sparks she was talking about? Perhaps he needed to go to a mechanic and have his spark plugs checked.

'You're a really nice guy and I enjoyed meeting you. I hope we can be friends.'

'Yes, me too.'

He didn't need a friend. He needed a wife. A friendly wife of course – or even a wifely friend. But not just a friend. He had enough friends: work friends, home friends, old friends, new friends, real friends, Internet friends.

After hanging up the phone, he consoled himself by drinking a Coke and watching the movie *Valli*. He found great comfort in Rajini's words: *'Nee virumburavalai kattikiruthai vida unnai virumburavalai kattikittaa un vazhkkai santhoshama irrukkum.* (You'll be happier if you marry the one who loves you instead of the one you love.)'

13

IT HAD BEEN SEVERAL MONTHS SINCE BALA HEARD FROM ANY of his aunts and uncles in India, so when he spotted the grey envelope from Balakrishnan Aunty in his pile of mail, he opened it as soon as he was done scanning the Victoria's Secret catalogue. Inside were two photos and a letter.

My dearest nephew,
It is me, your Athai, writing to you. How you are?
Your mother is telling me you are doing well and
I am so happy. I am so joyful and proud to have
nephew who is big health director in America.

We all are doing fine. Your uncle is working a
little less these days, coming home as early as 8
p.m. He is able to do it because Shiva is working
with him now. Shiva is very much like his father,
very much dedicated to medicine. Even at home,
he is wearing stethoscope. I ask him what he is
listening and he say, 'Oh, just hip hop.' He is always
using medical terms.

Hari works in emergency department of Chennai
hospital. He likes to be in Chennai, I don't know why,
maybe because the disorderly traffic gives him lots
of patients. He is working seven days a week. On
Sundays, he gives free treatment to poor people.
I tell him to take rest, but he say to me, 'Amma, it
is my calling. Do you know that you can't spell the
word "charity" without 'hari'?'

Vani is finishing her B.E. in few weeks from
Tuticorin Tech. She is good student. You will be

happy to know that she is also exercising regularly, doing pushups and all. I tell her that girls should not have muscles and she say to me, 'Come on, Amma, how else am I supposed to lift those engineering textbooks?' I thought you would find it funny. I remember how you used to have that big book B.E. Made Easy.

Bala, I have question for you: When you are getting married? You must come to India to find bride. Population here is over one billion, so you will have many more choices here. We are also very much eager to see you. It has been too long since you left.
Your loving Athai.

Bala studied the two photos, one of Hari and Shiva standing in front of their father's clinic, the other of Vani sitting on the hood of a shiny blue Mercedes. Shiva was the spitting image of his father – he even had those wire-rimmed glasses from the Victorian era – but more remarkable than that, Vani had transformed herself into an alluring young woman, her hair spilling down over her shoulders like curtains, drawn open to a riveting show: teeth as white and inviting as a glass of lassi, skin like rich maple, and a pair of bulges in the V-necked blouse that Bala's eyes tripped over. A twinge of uneasiness swept through his body. She was his cousin, darn it, and the last time he saw her, she had just turned sixteen, the seven years between them gaping wider than her father's garage. But as he stared at the picture, held it under the dining room chandelier, marvelled at her striking beauty, his unease began to lift, melting away in the hard glare, until all that remained was pride – deep unabashed pride. The same pride that a brother might have for a sister. Pride that inspired – no, compelled – him to post her picture on his refrigerator door, where his friends were sure to see it – and just as sure to go nuts, especially Mike, who acted like female beauty was one of God's greatest gifts to mankind, not far behind beer and football.

With a Domino's magnet hugging her legs, Vani looked like a model on a billboard, the type who would cause major backups on the highway. Was this really the same demure girl he had watched growing up, the 3-year-old who had liked to go camping, mostly inside her mother's sari; the 9-year-old who had made plenty of friends, mostly within Enid Blyton books; and the 14-year-old who had finally started talking to boys, mostly to tell them to stop bossing their little sister around.

It was Thiru who first spotted the picture, first read the words Bala had inscribed on the border: 'My cousin Vani.'

'She's your cousin?' he asked, his fingers curled around the fridge handle. 'Very lovely. What do you think, Mike?'

Bala smiled as his lanky friend, watching *Lagaan* with John, Linda and her boyfriend, Miguel, scrambled off the couch so fast, he bumped his ankle against the coffee table. Wincing momentarily, he hobbled to the kitchen, nudged Thiru aside and let out a whoop. 'Holy shit, man! Who is this beautiful creature?'

'His cousin, yaar, didn't you hear?'

'Cousin?' Mike slid the picture off the fridge, held it under the point of his chin, scrutinized it like a biologist inspecting a rare specimen. 'What, man, you've been hiding her from me. This isn't fair at all. I was ready to set you up with my cousin, and here you are, keeping this lovely creature to yourself. Have you already proposed or what?'

'You crazy, Mike? She's like a sister to me.'

'Sister, kissed her,' Mike said. He pulled open the fridge and scanned the row of Heinekens and Cokes on the bottom shelf, as though he had a choice to make. 'Come on, man. Don't talk like you've never heard of cousin marriage, like you Tamils don't do it.'

'Hey, isn't that against the law?' John said, walking into the kitchen. 'I mean, it *is* in some states. But probably not in West Virginia.'

'Not in India either, man,' Mike said, grabbing his fourth Heineken. 'One of my second cousins, crazy girl, even married her uncle – her mother's brother. Now her children are also her cousins. Can you imagine?'

John shook his head. 'That would be strange.'

'Yeah, I know,' Mike said. 'It's better to marry your cousin, I say, especially if she looks like this.'

'Isn't there a risk of birth defects?' John asked. 'The children might be born with a third leg or something.'

'I've got a third leg,' Mike said, grabbing his crotch. 'That's the only birth defect in my family. Look, Bala, if you don't want her, just let me have a shot. I'll fly to India tomorrow if you want.'

'Go ahead, Mike,' Bala said, reaching out to reclaim Vani's photo. 'I'm sure my uncle will gladly give you a shot. Just tell him where you want it: in your arm or in your butt.'

They returned to the living room, having missed only a portion of a dance sequence. The Oscar-nominated movie, starring Aamir Khan and Gracy Singh, was one of Bala's all-time favourites. He enjoyed watching both movies and cricket, and this was a brilliant concept: a movie about cricket. He was already looking forward to

Lagaan 2, 3, 4 and *5*.

Three hours into the movie, at about 11 p.m., John yawned and asked, 'What inning is it?'

'I don't know,' Miguel said. 'They're probably playing extra innings. This movie is so freakin' long.'

'Only four hours,' Bala said.

'One hour of dancing, three hours of cricket,' John said.

'Four hours is nothing for a good romantic musical sports drama,' Bala said.

'If you say so,' Mike said. 'I just hope you don't run out of beer. It's the only way I'm going to get through this.'

'This story seems kind of familiar,' Miguel said. 'I feel like I might have seen it somewhere before.'

'No way,' Thiru said. 'Indian movies are 110 percent original. You must be thinking of a Mexican movie.'

'Mexican movies are 120 percent original! They're much better than this crap.'

'Oh yeah? Then how come Mexican movies aren't popular in Afghanistan?'

'You mean Indian movies are?'

'Of course! They're almost as popular as public hangings. Two Bollywood movies have even won the Kabul Film Festival's Well-Executed Award. What about Mexican movies?'

'Quit the yapping, guys, and enjoy the movie,' Linda said. 'The music and dancing are beautiful – and so is Aim Ear Can. Is he related to Share Rook Can?'

'No, they're not related,' Bala said. 'Khan is a common name in Bollywood. There's also Salman Khan and Saif Ali Khan.'

'Yes,' Mike said, 'and don't forget about Hrithik Rosh Khan and Amitabh Bach Khan.'

Bala laughed. Mike was such a joker. You could never take him seriously. Did he really want to go to India to marry Vani? Probably not. With her looks and qualifications, not to mention the small fortune Balakrishnan Uncle could afford to give as dowry, prospective grooms were likely camping outside their mansion. But why had Aunty sent him Vani's photo? Was she hoping he would join the line of suitors? He tried to imagine himself married to Vani. It would be strange, having Uncle and Aunty as in-laws. They would know so much about him, all the good deeds from his childhood, as well as the embarrassing ones. The last time he had visited them, just before leaving for America, Uncle had gone into one of his reminiscing moods, entertaining everyone at the dining table with a few stories from Bala's childhood, including one that Bala preferred not to remember. As Uncle told it, he had bought Bala a toy gun, one that fired plastic darts. Bala spotted a pigeon on a tree limb and managed to sneak under it. But before he could pull the trigger, the pigeon flew off, leaving a grey splotch on Bala's shirt. 'The pigeon is shooting him instead,' Uncle roared in his gravelly voice. Bala could only blush and wait for the laughter to subside. Uncle slapped his back and said, 'Well, at least you are shooting four other birds and none of them is shooting you!' Laughter erupted again. Hari banged on the table and tears came to Aunty's eyes.

Despite Uncle's stories, there were obvious advantages to marrying Vani. She was beautiful and would make Bala the envy of many men, including Mike. Except for his close friends, no one would need to know she was his cousin. Their families would save money on the wedding, because many of his guests would be hers too. They would share a set of grandparents, and their children would have no trouble tracing their roots. And they'd be keeping the wealth within the family. Uncle would give his nephew – not some stranger – his daughter's hand in marriage and the keys to his Mercedes. 'Take good care of her, Bala,' he would say. 'Don't drive her too hard.'

The movie ended around midnight and Bala's guests rose to leave. 'So what did you think?' he asked.

'Not bad at all,' John said. 'A little long, but not bad at all.'

'Very good,' Linda said. 'Lovely music and dancing.'

'Excellent,' Mike said. 'Smooth and not too filling.'

Bala looked in the fridge. All the Heinekens were gone. He dashed out after Mike, who was attempting to get into his Lexus. 'Mike, come back inside. You shouldn't be driving. You can sleep on the couch.'

'No, man... I'm fine.'

'No, you're not, Mike. You're about to get into the trunk.'

'No, I'm not. Look... there's the steering wheel.'

'That's not the steering wheel, Mike. That's the spare tyre.'

'Damn it! Where the hell's the front door?'

'Mike, come back inside. I have something to ask you about my cousin.'

'Your cousin?'

'Yes, my cousin Vani.'

Mike followed Bala inside and plopped down on the couch. 'What did you want to... uh... ask me?'

'It's about my cousin. Do you really think I should hook up with her?'

'No, man, I really think you should... I really think you should... what was the question again?'

14

WHEN BALA CALLED AMMA THAT SATURDAY, HE HOPED TO find out that Uncle and Aunty had inquired about him, that they were indeed trying to set him up with Vani. But before he could broach the subject, Amma said, 'I have good news and bad news.'

'Bad news? What bad news?'

'Oh, nothing to worry about, kanna. Rajan lost. He was third. But he has made big name for himself and is going to be making CD.'

Bala heard Appa in the background: 'Making CD? He is better at making beedi.'

'What's the good news, Amma?'

'Rajan is getting married to Vani.'

'What?' Bala hoped he had heard wrong.

'Your cousins are getting married. Rajan and Vani. Is it not great?'

'Yes, Amma, it's great. Fantastic.' It was so fantastic that Bala felt like punching the wall. How crazy was this – the good news was worse than the bad news.

'Rajan has liked Vani for long time, maybe three or four years. And Vani liked him too, when she saw him on TV. He is going to be making lot of money. They have even asked him to make music for Rajini film. Can you believe it? I am related to someone whose music is going to go inside Rajini's ears!'

'That's great, Amma. But I thought Uncle and Aunty would be looking for a doctor or engineer.'

'Yes, yes, they were thinking of you even. But Vani wants to stay in India. Rajan has promised not to leave Tamil Nadu. He is also promising not to smoke anymore and to shave daily. They are calling it pre-nuptial agreement.'

Bala looked at the date on his watch. Was it April Fool's Day? No, it wasn't even April. He felt a strange woozy sensation, as though his world had suddenly turned upside down. Rajan, who once looked like an utter failure, was now a big star and had won Vani's hand in marriage. It was like hearing that it had snowed in Chennai or that Appa had left the water running in the bathroom.

'When are they getting married, Amma?'

'August 20th. You must come for the wedding. We all want to see you.'

'No, Amma, I don't think I can.'

'Please, kanna, please. Come for the wedding and you can also meet some girls. I will find you...'

'Yes, I know – some nice, sweet ones that are not spoiled. I don't want you to do anything, Amma.'

'What is wrong with you? You don't want to get married?'

'I don't want *you* to arrange it. I want to meet someone myself.'

'You are the one who is going to meet the girls, no one else. We will only find the girls, you will meet them and you will decide. Final decision is up to you. No forcing.'

Bala could hear Appa again: 'Forcing is good. What is wrong with forcing?'

'I don't know about this, Amma.'

'What you don't know? What there is to know? Everyone is getting married like this. Look at Appa and me. We are happy. I did not even speak to him before marriage.'

Appa's voice came through again: 'That is what I

liked about you. But these days I cannot get you to keep quiet.'

'Oh, look who cannot be quiet now,' Amma said. 'Your Appa is crazy sometimes. We are not agreeing on many things, but we are always adjusting. When you marry, you too must adjust.'

It wasn't the first time Bala had been told to adjust. On buses and trains in India, he often had to adjust – shift to one side to allow another person to squeeze in. When he was cramming for an engineering exam and complained to the young man next door that his music was too loud, the man shrugged and said, 'I am having party. Can you please adjust?' Then there was the time in school when he walked into a classroom and Mr. Venkatesh, the mathematics teacher, pointed at his zipper and said, 'Please adjust yourself.'

Amma and Appa were indeed a well-adjusted couple. He was the model of thriftiness, intent on saving every paisa, but had adjusted to owning three TVs, mostly to appease his wife. She was eager to own a car – they could easily afford a small Maruti – but had adjusted to taking taxis and auto-rickshaws, as well as the occasional ride on his once-trusty, but now rusty two-wheeler. He was untidy by nature, rarely putting things back where they belonged, but had adjusted to the idea of screwing the cap back on the toothpaste. She had little interest in sports, could barely tell the difference between football and wrestling, but had adjusted to having cricket matches on TV, sometimes sitting beside her husband and making astute comments such as, 'Mahendra is not looking good today. I don't know who is cutting his hair.'

'I've done enough adjusting in my life, Amma.'

'No, kanna, you must keep on adjusting. All your life,

you must adjust. Look at your Thatha, how well he has adjusted to having no hair. Everyone adjusts. Now why you can't adjust your schedule and come to India?'

'Let me think about it.'

'What there is to think? Too much thinking is not good. Just buy ticket and come. You can meet the girls, choose one, then after few months, you can come back to get married.'

'What if I don't like any of them?'

'If you don't like, it is okay. But that is not going to happen. I will find good quality girls. A-plus-plus girls.'

Bala did not share Amma's optimism. But he wanted to see if he would have more luck in India than in America. As Balakrishnan Aunty had written, there were more eligible brides in India, millions more. Most of them, however, would have an easier time getting through security at Buckingham Palace than Amma's screening process. Bala tried to get Amma to list all the criteria, but all she said was, 'You don't worry, kanna. I know what to look for. I am your Amma, aren't I?'

The timing of the trip couldn't have been better. August was a slow month for Bala. The shipping department had assumed most of the load, hiring extra workers to keep up with all the orders for The Flexerciser. Every time an infomercial aired on a station somewhere – all 50 u.s. states, Puerto Rico and the lower half of Canada – the customer service department in India was flooded with calls. The once-stout Tifatny looked as slim as a flagpole as he sat on The Flexerciser and exclaimed, 'Wow, I just got on and I'm already sweating like a dog. What a great workout! And so relaxing too! I can do this in my sleep.' That gave Bala an idea for a new machine: The Flexsnoozer.

Slogan: 'Don't exercise during the day – just snooze your big butt away.'

When Bala told Mike he was going to India to attend Vani's wedding, his friend acted disappointed at first, then skeptical. 'Come on, man, you can tell me the truth. You're going to get married to her, aren't ya?'

'Only if the groom doesn't show up.'

'We can arrange that, you know.'

'What do you mean?'

'Well, he could have a little accident on the way to the wedding. I have connections.'

'Shut up, Mike. He's my cousin.'

'Aha! So it *is* a cousin marriage!'

'It's not a cousin marriage! Vani is my cousin on my mother's side and Rajan is my cousin on my father's side.'

'Is this the same Rajan from *Indian Idol*? The one you said was always smoking beedis?'

'Yes, it's him. He has promised to give up smoking.'

'Really? That's very wise of him. It reminds me of the promise I made my parents a few years ago.'

'To give up drinking?'

'No, man, are you crazy? To give up thinking. I used to spend a lot of time thinking about all sorts of things. For example, why do you have to be only 18 to vote, but 21 to drink? I mean, aren't we discriminating against people aged 18 to 20? Why are they the only ones who have to vote while sober?'

15

DURING HIS CONNECTING FLIGHT FROM FRANKFURT TO Chennai, Bala enjoyed chatting with a man in his late thirties named Vijay, who was making his annual trip home with his wife and two children.

'I hope I don't have any trouble at customs,' Bala said. 'I've brought many gifts. A suitcase full of dishes for my mother.'

'You must do what I do,' Vijay said. 'Just give $20 to an airport officer and he will take you straight through like a VIP. Sometimes you have to use Indian customs to get past Indian customs.'

Bala laughed, but he was reluctant to bribe anyone, to contribute to corruption. He didn't think of it as an *Indian* custom. Surely it was something the British brought with them, along with the political system, bureaucracy and those darned mosquitoes. It bothered him that corruption was still commonplace in India. He had once tried to stop Appa from bribing everyone – the old man would even slip an extra twenty rupees to the cable guy – but Appa wouldn't listen, saying, 'Without corruption, there is disruption.'

Bala thought of Appa's words as he stood in the never-ending line at the airport, waiting for his passport to be stamped and the customs officers to check his luggage. He would have liked to see a little disruption, instead of this orderly line that was creeping along at a snail's pace – an old, sickly snail that kept taking naps. It was only his first night back, but he knew that the three weeks would go quickly and he didn't want to spend an hour or two looking at someone's backside, not even a young woman's. He had watched Vijay and his family being led to the vip counter, sailing through in less than a minute, waving at Bala and making him feel like a complete idiot. He was tempted to follow their example, recalling what Rajini had said in *Annamalai*: '*Naan solrathaiyum seiyven, sollathathaiyum seiyven.* (I'll do what I say and I will do what I don't say.)'

More than an hour later, when he pushed his luggage cart onto the pavement outside the terminal, he was glad he hadn't bribed anyone. The customs officers hadn't bothered to look inside his suitcases, perhaps saving him thousands of rupees.

It was 12:30 a.m. and the airport entrance was quieter than usual, with only a few hundred people milling around. Many were waiting for passengers behind a metal barrier. A man called out to Bala, 'Sir, taxi, sir. Taxi, sir.' Another man shouted, 'Sir, auto, sir. Auto, sir.' A third man yelled, 'Sir, bullock cart, sir. Bullock cart, sir.'

Bala looked in the direction of the third voice and immediately recognized the man. It was Gopal, his friend from college, standing at the gate beside Bala's parents and sister, smiling broadly. 'Surprise!' Gopal said, shaking Bala's hand. Bala was indeed surprised to see him. They had exchanged a couple of emails over the years, but had not really kept in touch.

Amma and Chitra gave him hugs and kisses, while Appa dispensed with the greetings and merely said, 'Ready to go?' as though Bala had returned from a day trip to Pondicherry. Appa was a man of principles, believing that all the hugging and kissing should be done at home, when the taxi's meter wasn't running.

'Are you coming home?' Bala asked Gopal.

'No, it's very late,' Gopal said. 'My wife is waiting. I

will visit you tomorrow.'

He helped Bala load the luggage onto a minivan, then walked to his two-wheeler. Bala gave him a quick Rajini salute and joined Amma and Chitra in the back of the van, while Appa sat in front with the driver. As they weaved past cars, auto-rickshaws and scooters, Appa turned to Bala and said, 'You are eating good in Amricka, I see.'

'Appa!' Chitra said, shaking her head.

'Your Amma has been telling brides' families all about you,' Appa said. 'She has been telling them you are round as a well.'

'Well-rounded!' Amma said. 'Not round as a well!'

'All the same,' Appa said. 'The main thing is, he is round.'

'Appa!' Chitra protested again.

'It's not nice to say such things,' Amma said. 'Don't worry about your Appa, kanna. He is crazy sometimes. Not nice at all. So tell me, what is happening to your hair? Are you going bald already? Even your appa went bald only after 30.'

'Amma!' Chitra said. 'Leave him alone. He has just arrived and you are already saying these things.'

'What things?' Amma said. 'I am not saying anything.'

'I'm losing hair only after Bala was born,' Appa said. 'It is easy to lose hair when you have children.'

Bala touched the back of his head. 'Is it that bad?'

'No, da, not bad at all,' Appa said, without looking. 'There is nothing wrong with being bald. It is good thing, actually. You can save money on haircuts. I have saved thousands and thousands of rupees. Better to have money in the bank than hair on the head. You can earn interest in the bank, but there is no interest in hair. Even your Amma has no interest in my hair – only her own.'

Bala and Chitra looked at each other and laughed. He was happy to see her, happy to have her support. She was the only one who understood what he had to endure, what it was like to have to deal with Amma and Appa since birth. Chitra had not changed much in five years, though she was a mere teenager when he left and now a full-fledged woman. She was entering her final year of college, studying to be a fashion designer. Amma and Appa had not expected her to become a doctor or engineer – only to marry one. Whenever Appa showed the slightest concern about her career choice, she reassured him by calling herself a 'soft-wear engineer'. Amma, for her part, was proud of both children. One was always making an impressive fashion statement, while the other had an impressive bank statement.

'Tomorrow, you will meet the first girl, kanna,' Amma said.

'So soon? I need to get some rest. It was a long trip.'

'Rest? What you were doing on the plane? Running around?'

'He will have jet leg,' Appa said.

'Jet *lag*, Appa,' Chitra said.

'I will have jet leg too,' Bala said. 'I could not stretch my legs on the plane.'

'Don't worry, kanna,' Amma said. 'You are meeting her in the evening only. You will have plenty of time to rest. After that, you will meet the girl who is coming all the way from Dubai to meet you.'

'She is flying here,' Appa said, just in case Bala thought she was coming by train.

'When am I meeting her?'

'The next evening.'

'That soon? I'm going to be here for three weeks, Amma. You could have spaced it out.'

'Don't be stupid idiot,' Appa said. 'Your Amma has arranged for you to meet three girls in three days. After that, you can relax, make your decision and start the wedding plans. Your Amma does what she is knowing.'

'Knows what she is doing,' Chitra said.

'All the same,' Appa said.

Three girls in three days. Bala felt like he was on a reality show. Was this the Indian version of *The Bachelor*? Would one girl end up feeling like the winner, while the others felt like losers? Who would be the biggest winner – Bala, his bride or Amma?

He struggled to fall asleep that night, partly because his body clock hadn't adjusted to the time difference and partly because the idea of meeting three women intimidated him. He told himself not to think of them all at once, to just take it one woman at a time. One woman at a time. He tried to picture just one woman, but kept seeing three, each trying to pull him toward her. The first woman grabbed his right ear, the second grabbed his left ear, and the third grabbed him where it hurt most.

He finally fell asleep around 4 a.m. and was out like a bear until noon, waking up groggily to the sound of Amma's voice. 'Gopal is here,' she said. 'He wants to take you to Bonda King for lunch.'

They rode to the vegetarian restaurant on Gopal's two-wheeler, as they had done countless times during college. Traffic was heavier and more chaotic than Bala remembered it. A three-kilometre ride took them almost 15 minutes and would have taken longer had Gopal not managed to squeeze between a bus and a cow. The cow was sitting beside the median, seemingly oblivious to the array of traffic passing it – cars, bicycles, scooters, motorcycles, auto-rickshaws, vans, trucks, and armoured tanks – not to mention the incessant beeping. Beep, beep, beep – it never stopped. Bala was certain that some drivers, worried about straining their fingers, had programmed their horns to blare every three seconds.

The number of cars and two-wheelers seemed to have doubled since Bala lived there, while the roads seemed to have narrowed. To get to their destinations on time, motorists were resorting to all sorts of manoeuvres. They didn't just tailgate – they side- and head-gated too. They made turns in the face of oncoming traffic. They weaved around potholes, trees and pedestrians. Bala, now accustomed to American driving, was amazed at the widespread indifference to personal safety. Few motorcyclists wore helmets; even fewer drivers wore seat belts. But many motorists did have pictures of gods and goddesses in their vehicles, so there was at least some much-needed praying going on.

When they arrived at Bonda King, Bala was glad to see that it had not changed at all – even the menus were the same, with new prices stuck over the old ones. The restaurant specialized in bondas – potato bondas, egg bondas, kosher bondas – but offered many other choices. Bala ordered the Madras thali, his very own mini-buffet, while Gopal, as usual, got himself a masala dosa, one that was thin, crispy and as wide as Sri Lanka.

'Same old Gopal,' Bala said. 'Nothing has changed.'

'Same old Gopal, except I'm having a boss now.'

'How long have you been married?'

Gopal laughed. 'I'm talking about the other boss. The one at home is cool.'

He had met his wife, Madhuri, at a music concert. They had been married for 10 months and were expecting their first child.

'You are hoping for a boy?'

'Boy, girl, it doesn't matter to me. India needs girls; otherwise the boys will have to marry each other. Then the population will stop growing. We need to beat China in something, no?'

'Don't worry. We are beating them in spelling contests.'

While they chatted, catching up on each other's life, two waiters hovered over their table like flies. Every time Bala took a sip of water, one of the waiters refilled his tumbler. All he had to do was look at the tumbler and the waiter stepped forward, getting in position to refill it.

'How friendly is America?' Gopal asked.

'Very friendly. You can even pull his tail and he won't bite you.'

'No, I mean the country. How friendly are the people?'

'Very friendly. They are just like us, but without any knowledge of cricket.'

Bala was impressed with the service at the restaurant. He had experienced it growing up, but now had a new appreciation for it. India, with its cheap labour, was truly a country of customer service. The service was even better at the Sunilco Petroleum Station, where Gopal stopped on the way back. Three uniformed attendants rushed to serve him. The first opened his tank, the second filled it up and the third helped him close his jaw after he saw the total price.

Bala had spent half the afternoon with Gopal and was starting to get anxious. He needed to get ready to meet the prospective bride.

'Good luck,' Gopal said, dropping Bala off. 'Don't be nervous. It is the girl who should be nervous, not you.'

Bala nodded, but knew he'd be nervous. It was bound to be awkward, meeting a stranger who might end up being his wife. He had tried to get Amma to describe the first prospect, but all she said was, 'Her name is Latha, she is software engineer, very beautiful, nice personality.' Career, looks, personality – that covered it all, apparently. Amma wouldn't say more, perhaps because she didn't want Bala to make any preconceived judgments.

Bala spent a whole hour getting ready, almost as long as Amma. He didn't trim his moustache this time; instead, he tried to fluff it up with a brush. He combed the hair on top of his head sideways, trying to cover as much of his bald spot as possible. He wore a navy blue suit that seemed to conceal his belly. He slipped on a pair of brown wingtip shoes and, upon Amma's suggestion, walked to a nearby store, where, for only Rs. 5, two shirtless old men polished them to a fine glow, each man taking one shoe and rubbing it vigorously with a cloth. Four other men were working in the store, all buffing customers' shoes. As he was leaving, Bala noticed that the slogan of a previous government was displayed on a banner in front of the store: 'India is shining.'

Bala felt like he was going to a job interview, one that somehow required him to bring his parents along. They squeezed into an auto-rickshaw and headed to Kumaran Colony in Vadapalani, where Latha lived with her parents. Bala, sandwiched between Appa and Amma, wished they had hired a taxi. Appa had insisted on an auto, saying it was cheaper and easier. 'Don't we have to impress them?' Bala had asked. Appa scrunched his nose and shook his head. 'You are in Amricka. What more there is to impress?'

Appa had spent a couple of minutes haggling with the auto driver, a young man in a khaki uniform, bringing the price down from Rs. 60 to Rs. 50. Bala wondered if it was worth the trouble, bargaining to save Rs. 10. Now that he worked in America, Rs. 10 seemed like a negligible amount, converting to only 25 cents. He could earn ten times that amount just reading a matrimonial ad at work. But of course Rs. 10 carried more purchasing power in India than 25 cents did in America. You could get a piece of jackfruit for Rs. 10, while for 25 cents, you couldn't get jack.

As they approached Latha's house, Amma volunteered a few more details: Her father, Mr. Srinivasan, was a district judge. Her mother was a librarian. She had two older brothers: one was an architect, the other an engineer. One of her uncles was a research scientist in America.

'He is working in Howard University,' Appa said.

'*Harvard* University,' Amma said.

'Howard. That is what I said,' Appa said.

'What about *her*?' Bala asked. 'Tell me about *her*.'

'It is about her only I am telling,' Amma said.

'What are her interests?'

'Interests? She is interested in getting married. What more you want to know?'

Before Bala could answer, the auto stopped in front of Latha's two-storey house. Her parents were waiting on the veranda, seated on rattan chairs. Bala felt his heart palpitate. Mr. and Mrs. Srinivasan greeted them with namastes and led them into a spacious living room with more rattan furniture and a rubber plant that was so tall and broad, Bala wondered if they were tapping it.

'So you are the big man from America!' Mr. Srinivasan said. He spoke with a booming voice, making Bala feel like he was sitting in a courtroom.

Bala hesitated, then said, 'Small man from India, actually.'

Mr. Srinivasan roared, displaying a gap in his upper teeth. 'Is that so?'

'He is just being modest,' Mrs. Srinivasan said. Her voice was soft, making Bala feel like he was sitting in a library.

'Every year, he is getting bigger,' Appa said, causing Bala to glance down at his belly. Was it protruding? No, the suit jacket was doing a good job of concealing it.

'How was your flight?' Mr. Srinivasan asked.

'Very good,' Bala said. 'The service was excellent.'

'You didn't take Air India? Why not?'

Bala was about to chuckle – it was just like a judge to draw such a quick conclusion – but Mr. Srinivasan's interrogational tone made him stifle it.

'It was overbooked,' he said. 'Air India was my first choice. If Indians don't fly Air India, who will?' He was glad he wasn't under oath.

Mr. Srinivasan seemed to like Bala's answer. He smiled and said, 'Yes, that is what I'm always saying. Indians need to support Indian institutions. Otherwise, how they are going to survive?'

'It is my philosophy too,' Appa said. 'That is why I am always using Indian trains. It is best transportation in the world.'

Mrs. Srinivasan rose to get some coffee. She reappeared a minute later carrying a tray of silver cups. Behind her was a young woman holding a plate of cake.

'This is my daughter, Latha,' Mr. Srinivasan boomed, loud enough for everyone in Bangladesh to hear.

Latha smiled, barely showing her teeth. She was light-skinned, with a small nose and round face. An elegant turquoise sari covered her slender body, from which a pair of twigs jutted out and grasped the plate.

After serving slices of the marbled cake, she sat in a chair next to her father.

'She has baked the cake herself,' Mrs. Srinivasan said.

'It is very good,' Amma said, without taking a bite. 'Not so, Bala?'

'Yes, very tasty.'

'Very exhalent,' Appa added. 'First-class cake.'

'She is good at cooking everything,' Mrs. Srinivasan said.

'Perfect!' Appa said. 'Bala is good at eating everything.'

Mr. Srinivasan roared, drowning out everyone else's laughter. 'What you like to eat?' he asked.

'He is strict vegetarian like us,' Amma said.

Bala didn't say anything. He *was* a strict vegetarian, most of the time.

'It is hard in America, no?' Mrs. Srinivasan said.

'Yes, very hard,' Amma said. 'Americans are eating everything, even worms.'

Bala frowned and shook his head.

'Yes, yes,' Amma said. 'I'm seeing it on TV.'

'Everything on TV isn't real, Amma.'

'No, it is real. I'm seeing it on *reality* show.'

'Reality?' Mr. Srinivasan said. 'What Americans know about reality? They are searching Iraq for weapons of mass destruction, but no one is searching Pakistan.'

Appa joined him in laughter, while the women smiled cautiously at each other.

A few minutes later, Mr. Srinivasan set his coffee cup down and asked if they'd like to see the garden in the backyard. Bala stood up, but Appa glared at him and he sat back down. He realized what was happening. The parents were leaving for a few minutes, so Bala and Latha could talk to each other. He had not even heard her voice yet. Controlling his nerves, he tried to get a conversation going, but Latha kept giving him short responses, her voice as soft as her mother's.

'How did you make the cake?'

'Flour.'

'Do you grow anything in the garden?'

'Flower.'

'What do you like to eat?'

'Idli.'

'Is there any country you'd like to visit?'

'Italy.'

'What part of Italy?'

'Rome.'

'What would you like to do there?'

'Roam.'

She didn't ask him any questions, just answered his with as few words as possible. It made him think longingly about America, with whom he had enjoyed longer and deeper conversations.

Thankfully, his parents returned within 10 minutes. Amma and Appa looked expectantly at Bala, as though they wanted him to give them a 'thumbs up' sign or something. Bala tried not to show any disappointment. He didn't want the judge to find him in contempt of court.

On the way home, Amma raved about Latha. 'Very

fair girl.'

Bala shook his head. 'That's all we're looking for?'

'Not all we're looking for, kanna. She is beautiful, that is all I'm saying.'

'She hardly spoke to me.'

'Don't worry, she will talk to you after marriage,' Appa said. 'Just like your Amma. Before marriage, I was not sure if she has a tongue. Now, I am not sure if she has just one.'

16

AFTER DRIVING A CAR IN AMERICA, BALA DID NOT LIKE THE idea of continually haggling with auto-rickshaw drivers for the privilege of being crammed with his parents. He wanted to rent or borrow a car, at least until he was done visiting all the women. He called his cousin Hari to see if he had an extra vehicle. Hari owned both a Honda Accord and a Suzuki motorcycle, but seemed hesitant to lend the car.

'Just for a few days,' Bala said.

'A few days?'

'Yeah, just two or three days. Come on, Hari. I'll take good care of it. I'm sure you already know this, but you can't spell the word "sharing" without "hari".'

Hari laughed. 'Oh, all right. Since you put it that way.'

Appa and Amma were not keen on the idea. 'This is not Amricka,' Appa said. 'You cannot drive here.'

'If you are having serious accident,' Amma said, 'no one will marry you.'

Their doubts about his driving skills made him even more determined to drive. Though it was late evening, more than two hours after they returned from Latha's house, he took an auto to Hari's apartment in Nungambakkam to pick up the car. Hari lived in a fancy apartment complex with elevators, a security guard and a sign that said, 'Fancy Apartment Complex'.

'What happened to Mr. Nine-dulkar?' Hari asked. 'Didn't I tell you that you need to gain height, not weight?'

He said it in such a good-naturedly way that Bala

didn't mind at all. 'It's all that American food. Too fattening.'

'So that's why you're eager to get married! You want to get some sexercise.'

Bala laughed and gave Hari a playful punch on the shoulder. Seeing his cousin rekindled fond memories of all the good times they had shared. It was like meeting a long-lost brother. They enjoyed several more laughs as they reminisced about the old days while drinking some wine.

When Bala was ready to leave, he expected his cousin to just hand him the car keys, but instead Hari led him downstairs to the car port, where a dhoti-clad young man was wiping the windshield with a wet cloth.

'This is my driver, Vivek,' Hari said. 'He will take you everywhere.'

'No, Hari, I don't need your driver. I just want the car.'

'No, no, no. You must take the driver. The car comes with the driver.'

'I always with car, sir,' Vivek said. 'If you wanting to drive, then I sitting in back.'

'Where will you sleep?'

'No problem, sir. I sleeping in back or in front.'

'Vivek, is very flexible,' Hari said. 'Aren't you, Vivek?'

Vivek put the cloth down and touched his toes. 'Yes, very flexible, sir. Because of yoga, sir.'

Bala smiled. 'Okay, then. Vivek is probably a better driver than I am.'

But he couldn't have been more wrong, as he realized on the drive home. Vivek was a terrible driver, one of the worst he had seen. Not only did he make turns without signalling, he made signals without turning.

He followed a truck right through a red light. He almost ran over a stray dog, then complained that dogs should not be on the pavement.

Passing a bus, he drove too fast over a pothole, giving Bala a jolt.

'Sorry sir, I liking Chennai so much.'

'What do you mean?'

'I liking Chennai so much, I forgetting about bad roads.'

Bala was relieved when he arrived home. It was like having a safe landing after a turbulent flight. His parents were in the sitting room, Amma watching a serial on TV, Appa reading *The Hindu*.

'What a drive!' Bala said, shaking his head.

'That is what we are telling you,' Amma said. 'Very difficult to drive here.'

'I didn't drive. Hari gave me his driver. I don't know whom he bribed to get his license.'

'Oh, he must be son of your uncle's old driver,' Amma said. 'I heard about him. He can take Hari to hospital very fast.'

'That is what I'm afraid of,' Bala said.

Appa burst out laughing. 'Very funny!' he said, his body shaking. Then Amma started laughing too, giggling uncontrollably.

'What's so funny?' Bala asked.

'I don't know,' Amma said. 'I start laughing because he is laughing.'

'This cartoon,' Appa said, passing the newspaper to Bala. 'Whoever is drawing that, he always is making me laugh.'

Bala looked at the editorial cartoon and laughed too. It showed U.S. Secretary of State Condoleezza Rice stepping off a plane in New Delhi to begin an official visit, a large crowd welcoming her. A man in the crowd is saying, 'Where is the rice? They told us we'd be receiving rice.'

As Bala was handing the paper back to Appa, he noticed the signature near the bottom of the cartoon: *P. Matthew*. His eyes popped. Could it be? No, there were probably thousands of P. Matthews in South India. But Priya had wanted to become a cartoonist. Perhaps she had achieved her ambition, drawing for one of the top newspapers in India.

'P. Matthew. Maybe this is Priya, my friend from school.'

'Don't be stupid idiot,' Appa said. 'This is not a girl. This is someone who knows all things about politics. Always drawing different things about politics, always funny.'

'Women don't know anything about politics – is that what you're saying, Appa?'

'You know better than that,' Amma said.

'No, I'm saying this is someone who is having sharp political mind of a man only.'

Appa was so sure of himself that Bala was determined to find out the truth. He didn't want to miss an opportunity to prove Appa wrong.

The next morning, he called *The Hindu*'s main number and asked for the Cartoon Department.

'There is no department like that,' a female voice said.

'Then can I speak to P. Matthew, your cartoonist.'

'P. Matthew. Hold on please.'

He was transferred to a subeditor, who said, 'Sorry, she works at home.' Bala had never been happier to hear the word 'she'. Even if it wasn't Priya, it was a woman and that made Appa WRONG.

'Can you tell me if her name is Priya? '

'That and all, I don't know. You can contact her if you want. Her email id is cartoons@shakespriya.com.'

'Thank you so much!' Bala said, excited to hear the email address. It *was* Priya!

He sent her a short email, asking her to call him. When the phone rang a few minutes later, he was certain it was her.

'Shakespriya!'

'Is it Bala? What are you saying?' Appa's voice was unmistakable.

'Nothing, Appa.'

'What language you were speaking?'

'Uh... Swahili.'

'Why you are speaking Swahili? This is India, not... not... Swahililand.'

'Sorry, Appa, I thought it was my friend calling from... uh... Swahililand.'

He didn't tell Appa that the cartoonist was Priya. He wanted to wait until he could see the look on Appa's face.

The phone rang again at about 4 p.m., just as Bala was entering the bathroom, about to get ready to meet the Dubai woman. This time, it was indeed Priya.

'Shakespriya! I can't believe you're still using that name after all these years.'

'Well, it's better than the name I got in college when I acted in my first play: Priyashakes.'

'So you're a big cartoonist now. My father loves your cartoons.'

'He does? That's nice to know. I'm not that big – though my father sometimes calls me R.K. Laxwoman.'

Bala had grown up reading the cartoons of the

legendary R.K. Laxman, which had inspired Bala, as a ten-year-old, to try his hand at drawing. But his depiction of Gandhi didn't impress anyone, not even Amma, who stared at it for a minute or two and asked: 'Rajiv or Indira?'

'It's been a long struggle, getting my cartoons in newspapers,' Priya continued. 'What about you – have you directed any movies yet?'

'Yeah, right,' Bala said. 'The only thing I've been directing these days is my dog.'

Priya laughed. 'Remember ABC? I'm still waiting to see it on a movie. I'm still waiting to scream, "I know that guy! I know that guy!"'

'Maybe someday. It's still a dream of mine.'

'So what brings you to India? Just visiting your family?'

'My cousin is getting married. I'm also meeting a few potential brides. You know the drill.'

'Ha! I went through that last year – met three guys. They were all – how can I put it nicely? – assholes.'

'Really?'

'Well, two of them definitely were. The third was just an ass. My father was a little upset that I wasn't interested in any of them. "One boy doesn't even want dowry," he said. And I said, "That's because *he* should be giving me dowry!"'

Her mother had died three years ago of ovarian cancer and ever since then, her father, a retired family planning official, had been in poor health, she said. 'Liver, pancreas, heart – it's just one thing after another. I've told him to stop drinking, but he has to have his whiskey every evening. Sometimes, when he isn't looking, I drink a little from his bottle, just to make sure he doesn't finish it all.'

'How thoughtful of you.'

'Yes, it's too bad he doesn't drink wine or I'd help him even more.'

Bala invited her to visit him that Saturday, after he was done seeing the prospective brides. 'That way, you can meet one of your fans,' he said. 'I want to surprise him.'

It was Appa who surprised Bala first. He brought home a box of mouth-watering Tirunelveli halwa. It had been years since Bala tasted the sweet and he quickly opened the box and started to cut himself a piece, when Appa shouted, 'No, not for you. It is for the girl.'

The girl's name was Ramani. She had a B.Com degree and worked in a bank. Her parents, Mr. and Mrs. Kumar, were business people.

'They are rolling dough,' Appa said.

'They have a bakery?' Bala asked.

'No, Appa means they are rolling *in* dough,' Chitra said. 'They own a big jewellery store in Dubai.'

Hari's car had space for five people, so Chitra decided to tag along. She hoped to write about the experience in her blog, while Amma and Appa hoped she'd learn something for her own not-too-distant marriage. But Chitra got an experience she hadn't bargained for: Vivek's driving. During the 35-minute trip to Ramadas Inn, where the Kumars were staying, Appa looked tense, Amma looked troubled and Chitra looked terrified. The two women even screamed in unison once, when Vivek almost struck a motorcycle, almost knocked down the six people on it. They were apparently going too slow for him. He slammed his brakes and swerved at the last instant, then stuck his head out the window and shouted, 'Foolish fools! Motorcycle not for more than four people!'

It was a narrow escape, one that convinced Bala not to use Vivek's services longer than necessary. Vivek was unquestionably a reckless driver. The only question was: how long would he remain wreckless?

Everyone seemed happy to get out of the car and enter the elegant hotel. But when Bala stepped off the elevator on the fourth floor, he felt tense again. His confidence in his appearance, in his ability to conceal his belly and bald spot, had suddenly diminished, all because some idiot had chosen to put mirrors on all sides of the elevator.

Fortunately, Ramani was far more outgoing than Latha and quickly put him at ease. She welcomed his family with a big smile, ushered them into a well-furnished suite and introduced them to her parents. She seemed an inch or two taller than Bala, and he was relieved to see that she was well-heeled, in more ways than one. Wearing a floral-pattern sari, she was a walking jewellery store, with gold and diamonds everywhere. The makeup on her face looked like it had been applied by a professional, someone who painted walls for a living.

'What part of America do you live in?' Mr. Kumar asked.

'Pennsylvania.'

'Ah yes, Pennsylvania. That's near Philadelphia, isn't it?'

'Yes, very near. You can't go to Philadelphia without passing through Pennsylvania.'

'I know a lot about America. I have never been there, but I know a lot.'

'Daddy's always watching the news,' Ramani said.

'So how was your flight?' Mr. Kumar asked.

'Great. The service was excellent.'

'That's good. We don't fly Air India either.'

'Good service is important,' Appa said. 'That is my philosophy.'

There was a loud knock on the door. 'Room Chervish!'

A man dressed in white brought them steaming chai, bondas and bajjis. Mrs. Kumar helped him serve everyone. Appa ate a bonda while sipping his chai, then looked around and said, 'Nice hotel.'

'It has a nice lounge,' Mr. Kumar said. 'Would you like to go and see?'

All the parents stood up together, as though their exit had been choreographed. Amma motioned Chitra to the door. She grabbed a bajji and joined them. Ramani smiled at Bala, a glass table separating them.

'I hear you're a big director. You must be making a lot.'

'Not a lot, but pretty good. I can afford a car, a house and a dog.'

'A dog? Can't everyone afford a dog?'

'Not in America. It's cheaper to have children. You can't claim your dog as a dependent. Otherwise I'd have a bigger tax refund and a lot more money saved in his college fund.'

Ramani smiled. 'So what kind of car do you drive?'

'A Toyota.'

'Really?' She furrowed her brow. 'Our maid drives a Toyota. I drive a Jaguar. It's Daddy's, but he lets me use it. Tell me about your house. How big is it?'

'Not too big. It has three bedrooms and 1 ½ bathrooms.'

'How many walk-in wardrobes does it have?'

'Uh... none.'

'Not even one?'

'Well, the wardrobe in my bedroom is fairly big. A mouse could walk in it.'

'A mouse? You have mice!' She put her hand over her mouth. 'I'm terrified of mice.'

'No, I don't have *mice*. I have only one mouse. He's always hanging around my computer.'

'Your computer?' She looked horrified. Then it dawned on her. 'Oh, that mouse! I don't mind that mouse. So how big is your sitting...'

'Listen, do you want to know about me or my house?'

'I already know about you. Your mother told us everything. She said you're a big fan of Rajinikanth, you like to watch cricket and your horoscope says you'll have a healthy and prosperous life.'

'My horoscope says that?'

'See, I even know things about you that you don't know yourself.'

They spoke for about twenty minutes. Then, during a lull in the conversation, their parents returned, along with a smiling Chitra. Bala wondered if they had been listening at the door. Appa and Amma looked pleased. They had apparently hit it off with the Kumars.

'Nice family,' Appa said on the drive home. 'Very nice family.'

'The girl is nice too,' Amma said. 'Not so fair like Latha, but quite fair. What you think, kanna?'

'What happened to "nice sweet ones that are not spoiled"?'

'What you mean? She is nice, she is sweet and she is little spoiled only.'

'Yes, and Rajini is little popular only.'

'What Rajini has to do with this?' Appa said. 'We are talking about Ramani. I think she is good one for you.'

'Good one for me? But I haven't even met the third one yet.'

'You will meet her tomorrow,' Appa said. 'Then, after that, you can make your decision, how soon you want to get married to Ramani.'

'Appa!' Chitra said.

'Don't force him,' Amma said, noticing Bala's pout. 'Let him make up his own mind that Ramani is best one for him. Let him decide for himself that third one is not so good as Ramani.'

17

THE THIRD ONE WAS A DENTIST NAMED SHILPA. HER FATHER, Mr. Sivakumar, was an accountant, her mother a schoolteacher. She had an older brother who worked for an Indian soft drink company called Gokacola. He had recently been promoted to assistant vice-president of marketing.

It was a long drive to their house in Adyar, and Bala was glad they had come in an auto. He was once again sandwiched between his parents, but at least his heart didn't keep jumping into his throat. Before sending Vivek back to Hari, Bala had asked Chitra if she wanted the driver to take her shopping.

'You can use my credit card and buy a few dresses,' Bala said.

'No thanks. My life is worth more than a few dresses.'

'What about jewellery?'

'If I had children, I would be tempted. But who will inherit the jewellery when I die?'

'Amma would.'

'Amma does not care about jewellery, only her precious dishes. If she could, she would hang those plates from her ears.'

Bala tried to picture Amma meeting the Sivakumars with plates hanging from her ears. They would immediately withdraw their daughter from consideration, not wanting her to marry into a crazy family.

As it was, *their* family was the one that appeared slightly crazy – at least initially. Shilpa and her parents were extremely fair-skinned, partly because they had emptied a bottle of talcum powder on their faces. They looked like they were auditioning for the Tamil version of *Night of the Living Dead*. Thankfully, Shilpa looked a little less ghostly than her parents, perhaps because they had reached the bottle before her.

Aside from the artificial skin tone, Shilpa had a pleasant face and long, luxuriant hair. She smiled often, displaying a set of slightly crooked, but gleaming teeth.

'So this is the big director we've heard so much about,' Mr. Sivakumar said.

'He is directing people in Amricka, China and India,' Appa said. 'Three continents.'

Bala didn't bother correcting Appa and neither did anyone else. They were too busy being impressed.

'We are always proud when we hear about Indians doing well in America,' Mr. Sivakumar said. 'We must show Americans what we are made of.'

'Yes, we must show them how great we are,' Appa said. 'That is my philosophy.'

'What is the name of that singer – Ravi Shankar's daughter?' Mr. Sivakumar asked.

'Norah Jones?' Bala said.

'Yes, she is great,' Mr. Sivakumar said. 'All you Indians in America, you must try to keep up with Jones.'

'I read about her in *The Hindu*,' Appa said. 'She has won eight granny awards.'

'Is she that old?' Mr. Sivakumar asked. 'No, it can't be.'

Bala and Shilpa, sitting at opposite ends of the room, looked at each other and smiled. They had made a small connection, even without exchanging a word. A short while later, when their parents went for a walk, Bala discovered that Shilpa had an attractive personality.

'You like America?' she asked.

'Yes, I do. But I miss so many things in India.'

'Like what?'

'Well, I miss the weather, especially when it's freezing over there. I miss the festivals, Deepavali, Pongal and all. And I miss all the small stores, the amma-and-appa shops. In America, everything has been taken over by big corporations. McDonalds, Starbucks, Wal-Mart – they're everywhere.'

'Just like Bonda King. They're starting to open them everywhere. We don't have Wal-Mart yet, but in many places, you can find a Dal-Mart. They sell every kind of dal there: toor dal, mung dal, sandal.'

'Someday, I'd like to make a movie about that – the owner of a small store losing his shirt to a large corporation. Maybe I can get Rajinikanth to act in it.'

'Everyone will want to see it – if Rajini is losing his shirt. Maybe you can put me in the movie too. I will be Rajini's daughter, the one who can't get married because her father has no money for dowry. I am very good at crying.'

'You are?'

'Yes, ask my parents. I even cried when I heard that Aishwarya's new movie isn't doing well in America.'

'Really? Are you a big Aishwarya fan?'

'No, I was hoping if the movie did well in America, she would move to Hollywood and leave Bollywood alone. Even I can act better than her.'

'You want to be an actress?'

'Who doesn't? I can be the next Suhasini. It was my ambition during my schooldays, but I became a dentist instead. I still do a bit of acting, whenever I need to scare my patients.' She pulled her lips into her mouth and pretended to be a toothless old woman. 'I didn't get my cavities filled when I was young and now I have one big cavity!'

Bala laughed. 'You're scarier than my dentist!'

'Thank you. I went to a good dental college.'

Bala was disappointed when his parents returned. He was enjoying his conversation with her. Of the three women he had met, he liked her the most.

'She seems nice,' he told his parents on the way home.

'Nice? Why you don't want "very nice"?' Appa said. 'You will get "very nice" if you marry Ramani – very nice dowry.'

'Dowry? I don't care about dowry.'

'Don't be stupid idiot,' Appa said. 'We will be giving dowry when your sister marries, so we must get dowry now. That is the system in India. We can't change it. We must accept it. Ramani's parents will give you very nice dowry. Big TV, fridge, washing machine, even Jupneze car.'

Bala had heard about men getting not just scooters and motorcycles, but even cars for dowry. While American grooms found themselves humming 'Here comes the bride' on their wedding day, Indian grooms found themselves singing 'Here comes the ride'.

'They will give you anything you want,' Amma said.

'Can they give me a nice wife? That is what I want.'

'Don't be stupid idiot,' Appa said. 'You must think very carefully. This is your only chance. After marriage, no one will give you big TV, fridge, washing machine, Jupneze car. You will have to play lottery to win these things.'

'Appa, I already have those things. I already have a

Japanese car.'

'If you don't want it, you can leave it with us. Your amma has been wanting car for long time, so she doesn't have to take taxi and autos. You can leave TV with us too. She has been wanting fourth TV for long time, so she doesn't have to take magazines to bathroom.'

'Don't be silly, Appa,' Amma said. 'I don't want fourth TV for bathroom. I want it for bedroom. Then I will have something to look forward to at night, other than your snoring.'

18

WHEN BALA OPENED THE DOOR THAT SATURDAY afternoon, he expected to see the girl who had often sat beside him in 11th and 12th Standard. But Priya looked so different, he thought for a moment she was a friend of Chitra's from college. He lowered his gaze and realized she wasn't a college student. She wasn't holding a cell phone, ready to push a button at any instant. She smiled and said, 'Bala!' She had a gleam in her eyes that was unmistakable. He spread out his arms and gave her a hug. 'Priya!'

'Oh my God, you look so different,' he said, leading her into the sitting room. Her hair was shorter, her hips wider, her cheeks rounder.

'So do you,' she said. 'You look good. Not so skinny anymore.'

He was pleased to hear that. It was the best compliment he had received that week. His cousin Arun had stopped by in the morning and said that he looked 'lighter and thinner'.

'Really?' Bala asked.

'Yes,' Arun said. 'Your moustache is lighter and your hair is thinner.'

Ponmani Aunty, Amma's cousin, had visited earlier in the week and also given him a compliment. 'America has been good for you,' she said. 'You have become nice and fat.' Bala had noticed that quite a few people in Chennai, including Ponmani Aunty, were overweight. They were part of India's growing middle class, the part that was growing with every meal. Some saw their weight as a positive thing, a sign of health and prosperity. Anyone on the street could be thin as a rail, but only the privileged could break the scale.

Priya seemed to have also gained weight, but looked good in her green salwar-kameez and polka dot dupatta. There was something about the way she carried herself, her air of confidence, that Bala found appealing.

'Your parents are around?'

'Yeah, let me get my dad.'

Appa was seated on the patio in the back, eating groundnuts and reading *The Hindu*. 'Appa, there's someone here to see you – the cartoonist you like.'

Appa jumped out of his seat. 'Yenna? What is he doing here?'

He followed Bala into the sitting room and looked bewildered as Bala said, 'This is my friend, Priya. We were in the same class in school.'

'Hello, how are you?' Appa said. Then he turned to Bala and said, 'Where is the cartoonist?'

'Oh, that's me,' Priya said, smiling.

'It's you?' Appa said, his eyes bulging. 'You are P. Matthew?'

'Last time I checked.'

Appa's forehead crinkled. 'Checked? Where did you check?'

'That's just an expression, Appa. She *is* the cartoonist.'

Appa shook his head and smiled at Priya. 'Sorry, I didn't know if he was joking. I have been reading your cartoons for long time. First-class cartoons. Crop of the cream!'

'Thank you.'

'How much they are paying you?'

'Appa!'

'It's okay,' Priya said, flicking her fingers to hush

Bala. 'They are paying me well, Uncle. But it helps that I get money from a few other newspapers too.'

'How you know so much about politics?'

'My father got me into it, Uncle. He is always talking about politics. Tamil Nadu politics, Kerala politics, even Bihar politics. He sometimes gives me ideas for cartoons.'

Appa smiled. 'Ah yes, your father is helping you. He is doing good job. I am always laughing at them. Ask Bala's mother. Let me get her.' He took a few steps toward the kitchen. 'Meena! Meena! The famous cartoonist is here.'

Amma came running out of the kitchen. 'R.K. Laxman? What he is doing here?'

'No, no, no,' Appa said. 'It is P. Matthew from *The Hindu*, the one who is always making me laugh.'

Amma spotted Priya and her mouth fell open. 'You are the cartoonist?'

'Yes, Amma, this is my friend Priya Matthew. She draws cartoons for *The Hindu*.'

'Oh yes, I remember you. You came to our house long time ago. What happened to your hair?'

'Amma!'

'It's okay,' Priya said, flicking her fingers again. 'I got it cut after college, Aunty. It was too curly.'

'You are married?' Amma asked.

Priya smiled. 'Not yet, Aunty.'

'Why not?'

'Amma!'

'It's okay. I haven't met the right person yet.'

'If you are not finding the right person,' Amma said, 'you must marry the left person – the person who is left. Then you must adjust. That is what I have been telling Bala also.'

'I don't want *left*overs, Amma.'

'Don't be stupid idiot,' Appa said. 'Ramani is not leftover.'

'He's just joking, Uncle,' Priya said. She scowled mockingly at Bala. 'Women are not leftovers, Bala! We are freshly cooked delicacies!'

'Sit down, sit down,' Amma said. 'I will bring you tea.'

When they were alone, Priya patted Bala's knee and said with a smile, 'I see you're still a stupid idiot. You must be the most successful stupid idiot in the world!'

He hadn't seen her in years, but it felt like they had been together all along. He half-expected her to pull out a pencil and draw a caricature of Appa.

'So who's Ramani? The woman you're going to marry?'

'The woman *they* want me to marry. She's from Dubai. Very outgoing but kind of spoiled. Not as nice as Shilpa, another woman I met.'

'So Shilpa's the lucky girl!'

'I don't know, Priya. It's a big decision. I have to live with it forever.'

'Only for one life,' she said, laughing.

'Yeah, but it might be fifty or sixty years. That's a long time to be married to the wrong woman. Come to think of it, that's a long time to be married to the right woman. Maybe I should just stay single.'

'I know what you mean. Being single has its pluses. You can do what you want. You don't have to listen to some jerk telling you how you're supposed to look after your dad.'

'What?'

'Those guys I met – you should have seen their reaction when I told them I want to take care of my dad, I want him to live with me. The first guy acted like I was insane. The second guy acted like I was on drugs. And the third guy acted like I was an insane woman on drugs.'

'What did your dad say about that?'

'He doesn't know that I told them that. He just wants me to get married. I turned thirty last month, you know, and in his eyes, I just passed the last stop on the train ride to spinsterhood. He thinks I should stop looking for Mr. Perfect and settle for Mr. So-so. To tell you the truth, Bala, I don't really want a guy who's good-looking, one of those John Abraham types. I mean, I'm no beauty queen, but I'd still like to be prettier than my husband. I don't want him to be drop-dead gorgeous, but I'd prefer it if he wasn't drop-dead ugly either. Any type of dropping dead is not for me. But he needs to have a good character. I'm not compromising on that. I'm not marrying some asshole who doesn't understand why I want to take care of my dad, why it's important to me. Dad says he'll live alone and be okay, but it just doesn't seem right to me. I mean, he has supported me all my life, Bala.'

Bala spotted a tear forming in her eye and moved closer to put his arm around her. 'Hey, what happened to the optimistic Priya I knew? I'm sure the right guy will come along.'

'He'd better,' she said, her face brightening. 'Because if he doesn't, I'm going to be very angry with him.'

They chatted for an hour, then Priya got up to leave. Amma popped out of the kitchen and asked her to stay for supper. But Priya said her father was waiting for her – she had already stayed too long. Bala walked her to the street corner. He hailed an auto for her and, waving off her objection, paid for her ride home. But just as the auto started to move, he shouted 'Wait!' and climbed in beside her. He wanted to spend more time with her.

'I'll take you home,' he said. 'We can talk some more.'

She smiled. 'You haven't changed a bit, Bala.'

'I hope you mean that in a good way.'

'Of course I do. Remember all those times you took the bus home with me? It was after that pervert touched me. You said you wanted to protect me and you showed me the moves you would use on anyone who came near me.'

'Rajini moves,' Bala said, slicing his arms through the air.

Priya laughed. 'I was hoping the pervert would show up again, just so you could beat him up.'

'I would have kicked him all the way to Hyderabad. And not the one in India.'

Priya smiled. She put her hand on his thigh and rubbed it gently. He put his hand on hers and rubbed back.

When he returned home, Amma was serving rice and puli kootu to Appa at the dining table, the sports page of *The Hindu* spread out in front of him.

'Where's Chitra?' Bala asked.

'Friends,' Appa said, making it sound like a contemptible word.

'Your friend – how old?' Amma asked.

'She just turned thirty. We're almost the same age.'

Amma lowered her head and shook it somberly. 'Poor girl. Thirty and not yet married. What is wrong with her?'

'There's nothing wrong with her, Amma. Her father is sick and she wants to take care of him. She's an only child. She wants him to live with her, even after marriage.'

'Oh no, that is too bad,' Amma said, shaking her head again. 'How she will get married? Which boy is going to agree to that?'

'Someone might,' Bala said. 'You never know.'

'Don't be stupid idiot,' Appa said. 'No one will agree to that. No one.' He sounded so sure of himself, as though he had just conducted a survey of every bachelor in India.

'I would.'

'What you mean "I would"?' Appa said. 'Anyone can say "I would" but marrying is different matter.'

'Okay then. I will. Is that better?'

Bala felt his lips moving, but wasn't sure who was uttering these words. They were coming from deep inside, a place where any respect for Appa's pronouncements had been trampled by Bala's desire to defend Priya. It was like a stampede, the cows running over the farmer, tired of having their milk stolen.

The room was quiet for a few seconds. Bala could almost hear Appa's blood boil. Then Appa erupted: 'What you mean "I will"? Are you saying you will marry her?'

'"I would" is better, kanna,' Amma said. 'We like "I would".'

Bala inhaled deeply. 'I like her, Amma.' He wanted to use the word 'love', but how would his parents understand that, when he himself didn't understand the feelings he had for her, feelings that had been pushed aside many years ago? He did know one thing: He wasn't going to let anyone hurt her, not his parents, not the pervert on the bus, not those jerks who couldn't figure out how special she was for putting her father's interests ahead of hers.

'But she... she is Malayali.'

'Don't worry, Amma. It isn't contagious.'

'Be serious!' Appa shouted. 'This is serious matter.'

'You said you want girl who is fair and slim. She is not fair at all. Very dark!'

'I did not say that, Amma! I said fairly slim!'

'She is not fairly slim,' Appa said. 'She is fairly fat.'

'I don't care about that anymore. Look at me – I'm overweight too. We can lose weight together.'

'She is Christian,' Amma said.

'Don't worry, Amma. I will still be Hindu.'

'What about your children?'

'They will be Chrindus.'

'I said "Be serious!"' Appa shouted.

'She is non-vegetarian,' Amma said. 'How you can marry non-vegetarian?'

Bala took another deep breath. 'Actually, to be completely honest with you, Amma... she is as vegetarian as I am.' One of their differences had become a similarity.

'What is her caste?' Appa asked.

'Uh... she's Ahuman.'

'Ahuman? I never heard of that. Is that high caste or low caste?'

'Very high caste, Appa. Very high caste.'

'What about dowry?' Amma said.

'Don't worry, Amma, I will buy you a fourth TV. A nice big TV, so it will look like Rajini is standing in your bedroom.'

'TV? I don't care about TV.'

'I will buy you a car also, Amma.'

'*You* are going to give us dowry?' Appa said. 'You really are stupid idiot!'

'It is his life,' Amma said. 'Let him spoil us... I mean,

let him spoil *it* if he wants.'

'What about her father?' Appa asked. 'You are going to take him to Amricka?'

'No, Appa, I'm going to move back here.'

The vein in Appa's forehead looked like it was going to burst. 'Stupid idiot! We educated you for nothing. You have brain, but you are not using it. You are suffering from brain drain.'

'Priya has a good job here, Appa. And I can get a good one too. India is changing. Look at all the modern technology.'

Appa shook his head. 'Modern technology? Because of modern technology, people are sending text messages to each other while standing in same line to get water.'

'I can't take Priya's father to America, Appa. He will have no health coverage. Medical care costs an arm and a leg over there. Here, it's only a finger and a toe.'

Appa sighed heavily. 'That is why you should marry Ramani. Then you don't have to worry about such things. Let them worry about it. Why should it be concern of yours?'

Appa's solution sounded so simple: marry Ramani, return to America and live happily ever after. There was only one minor problem: He didn't like Ramani. He liked Priya. He had been given a second chance with her and he didn't want to throw it away. America would always be there – it wasn't going anywhere – but Priya might marry someone else. And then what would he do – go to bed at night, cuddling his green card?

It occurred to him that he hadn't asked Priya to marry him. He had just assumed she would say 'yes'. But what if she turned him down? What if she, like Uma, had not felt any 'sparks'? The thought scared him, but then he remembered what she had said: 'So

Shilpa's the lucky girl?' Lucky. He was encouraged by
that, but then he remembered something else she had
said: 'I don't really want a guy who's good-looking.' He
went to the bathroom and looked in the mirror. Oh
no, he *was* kind of good-looking. He found a pair of
scissors and trimmed his moustache, combed his hair
forward to expose his bald spot, and stuck his stomach
out as far as it would go. That was better. Not so good-
looking anymore.

He called Priya and asked if he could visit her the
next day. 'Sure,' she said. 'Why don't you come for
supper? I always cook something special on Sundays.
Don't worry, it'll be vegetarian.'

He was surprised. 'Aren't you non-vegetarian?'

'Not anymore. I stopped eating meat three years ago.
For health reasons mostly. Not just for me, but also my
dad. He doesn't need the fat and cholesterol.'

'That's great, Priya. Everybody should be vegetarian.
It's so much healthier.' It was true. He really believed
that. And he told himself that he would try his best to
be a vegetarian again. If he could return to India, he
could certainly return to paruppu saadam.

The next day, soon after lunch, he hired a taxi and
visited the jewellery stores in T. Nagar. He bought
a twenty-two-carat gold necklace and a one-carat,
emerald-cut diamond ring, spending more than two
lakhs. He felt good about buying the jewellery; his only
regret was that Appa wasn't there to see him paying
for them. Appa had never shelled out so much, except
while eating groundnuts.

Bala took the jewellery out of their boxes, putting the
ring in his shirt pocket, the necklace in his pants. Then
he headed to Priya's house in Kodambakkam, stopping
along the way to pick up three bottles of Coke. He wasn't

sure if they'd help him, but he had already spent two lakhs, so what harm could another thirty rupees do?

Priya lived in an old bungalow her father had purchased in the late 1980s, one with a large verandah and a door that was barely taller than Bala. She answered his knock with a wide smile and a greeting that made him uneasy: 'Hey good-looking!'

She was in the midst of cooking and asked him to sit in the dining room, so they could chat while she finished. Pouring him some Coke in a blue-tinted glass, she said, 'My father is taking a short nap. He'll join us for supper. We're having vegetable biryani.' She went into the kitchen to check on the dish, which was emitting a zesty, mouth-watering aroma.

Bala wasn't sure how to give her the diamond ring and necklace. With her father napping, this was a good opportunity to surprise her, to put the jewellery in a place where she would find them. But he felt anxious, unsure of himself. What if she said 'no'? Droplets of sweat formed on his brow. He took a sip of Coke, hoping it would cool him, give him some confidence.

On the side wall, above a row of cabinets, was a wooden shelf holding a colourfully painted ceramic bowl, a glass vase with dried flowers, and a set of books. One was a biography of Mahatma Gandhi, another the History of the Indian Railways, and the rest all bore the same name: Rushdie.

'Who reads Rushdie?'

'My dad mostly,' Priya said from the kitchen. 'That's his favourite author. Those are all first editions. They might be worth something someday. Do you like Rushdie?'

'Yes, I'm working on...' He caught himself. 'I just bought one of his books, *Midnight's Children*, but haven't read it.'

'You'll love it. Brilliant book. Actually, "brilliant" doesn't do the book justice. It's superbrilliant. I've read it three or four times.'

Bala stood up and pulled out one of the Rushdies, a novel called *The Ground Beneath Her Feet*. He turned the pages, read a few sentences, marvelled at Priya's and Mr. Matthew's intellect. It was a huge book, about 600 pages. If Bala could somehow manage to read a page a day, it would take him less than two years to get through the novel, not to mention the dictionary.

He sipped the Coke, read another sentence, tried to figure out the meanings of 'mesmeric' and 'quotidian'. As he put the glass down, it slipped out of his hand and tipped over. The remaining Coke had an entire table to spill onto, but, like so many readers, decided to rush to Rushdie. In a panic, Bala grabbed the first thing he could think of to wipe it up: his shirt. He pulled the shirttail out of his pants, leaned over the table and dabbed at the book. But it was too late. The Coke had stained the edges of numerous pages and left a large splotch on the page Bala was reading. Bala closed the book hurriedly and put it back on the shelf, wondering if he had ruined it, if it had lost its value. Then he spotted a small puddle on the tiled floor. The Coke had dribbled off the edge of the table. He didn't want Priya to see it and fell to his knees to wipe the puddle with his shirt, scolding himself for being so clumsy. As he patted the shirt down, the ring slipped out of his pocket and rolled on the floor. He stretched forward to retrieve it and, just then, Priya walked into the room.

She saw Bala on his hands and knees, holding the ring, and screamed: 'Oh Bala! Oh Bala! Oh Bala!'

Realizing what was happening, he started to say

what he thought men say in these situations: 'Do you think you might consider...' But before he could finish, she screamed, 'Yes, yes, yes!'

She took the ring from him, looked at it closely and screamed some more: 'Oh Bala! Oh Bala! Oh Bala!' He hoped her father was sleeping soundly; otherwise he might think they were up to something.

He decided to keep the necklace in his pocket and give it to her later. The ring had caused enough excitement.

Priya slipped it on her finger, hugged him and then kissed him, first on his cheeks, then on his lips. 'I feel like I'm having a dream,' she said. 'That was so romantic of you, getting down on your knees and surprising me.'

'What can I say,' he said, suddenly brimming with confidence, 'I put the "man" in "romance".' He was glad he had also put his faith in Coke.

She kissed him some more, then suddenly pulled back. 'You know I can't come to America with you?'

'I know, Priya. I'm moving back here.' He pulled her into his arms again.

They were still holding each other when a door creaked and footsteps sounded in the hallway. Mr. Matthew, a greying man with a slight stoop, plodded into the room, his face gaunt and weary. 'What's all the noise? Can't an old man get some rest?'

'Achan, you won't believe it. Bala has asked me to marry him.'

Mr. Matthew's eyes lit up. 'Is that so? Oh, what good news. What splendid news.' He held out his hand for Bala to shake. 'Priya has told me so much about you.'

He hugged his daughter and kissed her on the forehead. 'Oh, how happy I am,' he said. 'This is the answer to my prayers.' Tears rolled down her cheeks and Bala's eyes welled up.

Bala Takes the Plunge

As Priya returned to the kitchen, Mr. Matthew took a seat and pointed at Bala's shirt. 'You are sweating so much.' Then he smiled. 'You didn't have to be nervous. She likes you very much. When you contacted her, she was very excited. But when she heard you were meeting other girls, she was very disappointed.'

Bala tucked his shirt back into his pants, concealing most of the Coke stain. Priya returned with a cup of tea and set it in front of her father.

'She has always looked after me,' he said. 'She is the best daughter and also the best son.'

He paused, choking up. 'She will be a good wife, just like her mother. She will give you many years of happiness.'

Bala nodded. He looked toward the shelf, spotted the Rushdie books and felt guilty about what he had done. He decided to own up to it. 'I was looking at one of your Rushdie books...' he started to say.

'You like them? They are first editions. I keep them in mint condition. I never bring any food or drinks near them.'

Bala gulped. 'Yes, they are in... uh... excellent condition.'

'Take them. It is my gift to you.'

'I cannot take them, Uncle.'

'No, please take them. It is my gift to my future son-in-law. They will give you many years of happiness.'

While Priya set the table, bringing out biryani, pachadi and brinjal, her father seemed to be deep in thought. 'How often you and Priya will be able to come to India?' he finally asked.

'Achan, I'm not going anywhere,' Priya said, taking a seat between the two men. 'Bala is coming here. He is going to live with us.'

Mr. Matthew smiled. 'Oh, that is wonderful, so wonderful.' He paused, rubbed his chin, seemed to be thinking again. 'But Bala, how you can leave America?'

Something clicked in Bala's head. It was true: how could he leave America? What was he thinking?

'You're right, Uncle. I can't leave America. I need to bring him here.'

Father and daughter looked at Bala like he had gone mad. He laughed. 'America is my dog. My Labrador retriever. I left him with my friend Thiru. I need to bring him with me when I move here. Would that be okay?'

'A dog named America? You're crazy,' Priya said, laughing. 'Of course, you can bring him. I love dogs and my dad loves America.'

'You do, Uncle?'

'Yes, yes, America is great. Wonderful country. They are spending billions of dollars to send people into outer space. One day, that will help India immensely. It is the only way we will solve our population problem.'

Priya smiled, shaking her head. 'My dad is still obsessed with his old job. He's always reminiscing about the good old days when India's population was only one billion.'

'Yes, it is true. Just a little while ago, I was thinking that if you and Bala settle in America, you will help reduce India's population by two. And maybe three or four, when you have children.'

'I can help India in other ways, Uncle. If I open a factory, I can give jobs to many people.'

'What about your dream to be a film director?' Priya asked.

'Maybe I can do that on the side.'

'On the side? Oh, you mean like playing Scrabble and

watching cricket! Bala, if you're going to do it, you need to take the plunge. You need to give it your all. That's what I did. I drew cartoons day and night. I was rejected hundreds of times. Remember how disappointed I was, Achan?'

'Yes, yes. I even told you, "Why don't you stop drawing cartoons and start drawing a paycheck?"'

'But I didn't give up. I kept on submitting my cartoons. The first thing you need to do, Bala, is enroll in Chennai Film Institute and study to be a director. We can live on my income for a few years, however long it takes for you to break into the movie industry.'

'You'll support us while I study?'

'Why not? I've achieved my dream, you deserve to achieve yours. It's only fair.'

'I've saved some money. We can live on that too.'

'You can spend that on your first movie. It's going to be a blockbuster, I'm sure, especially if it has Mammooty in it.'

'Yes, yes,' her father said. 'Mammooty is the best.'

Bala chuckled, resisting the urge to disagree, though he was certain Rajini was better. 'I don't think I can afford Mammooty. It's going to be a low-budget movie.'

'But I'm sure it will still be good,' Priya said, reaching over and rubbing Bala's hand. 'I'll be so proud to see a movie with your name on it.'

Bala looked at her face, the gleam in her eyes, the smile on her lips. He knew he had to do it. He had to give it a shot, not just for himself, but for this special lady, who was so willing to invest in his dreams. He squeezed her hand gently and smiled back at her, pleased that he was marrying a very fair woman indeed.